# Onyx

Onyx Series: Book 1

## Theo Mann

Invisible Publishing Company

# Contents

# Chapter 1

Ballantyne, Montana, 1865

Ida Blanchard raised her rifle to her eye and sighted down the barrel. She tightened her knees on her horse and steadied herself to fire.

The elk herd crested the hill beyond Ida's cattle. The elk trotted down the other side making for the stream at the bottom. Last of all came a huge stag. He rotated his antlers from side to side surveying the countryside with regal indulgence. When he determined the area was safe, he sauntered after his does at a leisurely pace.

Ida's stomach fluttered training her rifle at his shoulder. This would be the biggest animal she ever shot. Her horse shifted his weight to his other foot. Ida nudged her knee into him to signal him silently to stand still.

The buck moved away from her and picked up his pace for the stream. He bared his shoulder to her. She couldn't ask for a better shot. She kept her sights on him even when he broke into a trot to catch up with his does.

The elk herd paused halfway down the slope. They searched the far hill for any sign of danger, but they saw only the cattle. Ida stiffened. As long as she didn't move, they would come straight toward her.

The does started forward with the buck bringing up the rear. Ida gripped the trigger ready to fire when, without warning, a sudden burst exploded in her face. A massive black bubble erupted from nowhere. It popped out of the very air right in front of Ida's horse.

The horse reared with a fearful screech and the bubble slammed into it. The impact flung the animal over onto his back. Ida tumbled out of the saddle and barely wheeled aside in time to avoid the horse smashing down on top of her.

The bubble kept expanding out of all proportion. It flashed to a monstrous size in a split second. In the blink of an eye, it enveloped elk, cattle, and horse inside its shimmering black surface. Only the force of her fall hurled Ida clear of getting caught in it, too.

She rolled to a stop a few feet from the bubble's margin. She lifted her head to find the smooth, black surface hovering just inches from her nose. She scrambled to get farther away from it, but it wasn't expanding anymore.

She staggered to her feet a few yards off and choked for breath before she dared to examine it. Her heart pounded her ribs and her head spun so she could hardly think at all.

She straightened up and checked the surroundings. The giant ball of darkness covered the whole valley. Its opposite edge rose almost to the hilltop where the elk first appeared. The surface rippled and swirled with mysterious colors hidden in a sea of black. It looked like a soap bubble from the laundry tub, but black—blacker than the darkest shadow. Even the wavering colors appeared to be deeper shades of black on the inky ball.

The darkness wasn't completely opaque, though. Through the mirror surface, a scene of horror played out before Ida's shocked gaze. The cattle and elk had transformed into fanged monsters with narrowed, slit eyes. Instead of antlers, the enormous buck carried a chandelier of jagged blades on top of his head. Sparks flew from his hooves when each foot struck the ground.

Ida gaped in blank disbelief as the stag charged one of her cattle. He lowered his rack and skewered the cow through the side. The cow rounded on him thrashing on the blades and Ida's stomach turned when she saw the animal's face. She couldn't decide which was worse, the buck or the cow.

The cow let out a guttural bellow that echoed out of the bubble and across the valley. It cracked its fanged mouth, arched its back, and attacked the buck with hellish ferocity. Spikes bristled from the once-placid cow's neck and down its spine. Needle thorns sprouted from its tail and its hooves flexed like claws.

The stag reacted by tossing his head in the air and the cow flipped off his horns. The cow twirled in the air and dropped. He caught her on his horns and hurled her away into a mob of similar monsters. The elk and cattle engaged in a wholesale war with every transformed animal fighting everyone else.

Ida's horse got trampled in the stampede of demon creatures attacking each other with insane ferocity. The horse raised his gruesome head out of the middle of the battle. His bloodshot eyes rolled in their sockets and razor teeth protruded from his mouth when he roared in fury.

The next minute, the elk and cattle pounded him under hundreds of stamping hooves. He submerged and didn't rise again.

Even birds and insects caught inside the bubble joined the fray. Bumblebees changed into howling missiles of spiked fury. A bluebird cocked back his arrow wings and speared his needle beak at everything in sight.

The rifle Ida dropped when she fell off her horse soared through the mayhem. It fired at random in all directions. Ida stared in amazement as the action levered itself and the trigger jerked back without anyone touching it.

The gun sprayed bullets everywhere. It rotated in mid-air until it swung its barrel in Ida's direction. Shells pocked the grass chewing their way toward her. She sprang out of the way as a line of bullets stabbed the ground near her feet.

The next instant, the gun swiveled the other way. It fired into the creatures falling on each other in a murderous frenzy. It rotated in a complete circle. It would spin around again and Ida didn't want to be anywhere nearby when that happened.

She darted up the hill. She didn't stop running until she gained the crest. Only then did she turn back to look. Was it real? Did that deadly bubble really just appear out of nowhere?

It was still there. The rifle's report kept clapping across the valley. Bellows, screeches, and rumbles came from inside the bubble. No matter how long she stood there watching, it didn't go away. She didn't want to believe it, but it was all too real.

The rifle pivoted in her direction again, but an object like that couldn't aim itself. It didn't aim at all. Grass tore out of the sod as slugs hammered toward the stream and then disappeared inside the bubble again.

Ida shivered. What in God's name was that thing? She didn't have a weapon—not that one would do her any good against this threat. She needed a gun and she needed a horse. What happened after she got them, she had no earthly idea.

# Chapter 2

Marvin Powel strode out of his cabin on his five-thousand-acre Montana ranch. He started to untie his horse from the porch corner when he heard hoofbeats coming up the hill.

He looked and almost didn't believe what he was seeing. The rider charged straight for him with a rifle clutched bare in the right hand. He'd never seen a rider like this in his life.

The person was definitely a woman. She wore a dress. Her skirts, petticoats, and her long, curly brown hair streamed out behind her in the wind, but she wore a man's battered cowboy hat tied under her chin.

She also wore a man's canvas work pants. Marvin wouldn't have been able to see them if she'd been standing on the ground. As it was, the wind lifted her skirts so he could see them and the unmistakable cowboy boots underneath. She even wore spurs and leather chaps under her dress.

She urged her horse to run faster. She didn't slow down even when she charged right up to the cabin. The horse huffed for breath and a swath of foam stained its shoulders and flanks from running hard.

The woman yanked the reins and the horse skidded in the dust. It squealed in alarm, but the woman paid no attention. She pitched the reins away and hurdled off the saddle with practiced ease.

Marvin stared at her storming toward him. Her face would have been beautiful if she wasn't glaring at him in lethal fury. She compressed her lips and her blue eyes flashed fire. Before he knew what to do or say, she whipped her rifle to her shoulder, jacked down the action, and sighted for his face.

Marvin's hand flew to his sidearm. "What the hell do you think you're doing?"

He got his pistol halfway out of its holster, but she didn't stop. She barged right up to him and that white rim across her knuckle told him all he needed to know. Her finger tightened around the trigger.

He'd never drawn on a woman before, much less shot at one. Ancient habit took over and he ducked to avoid the shot. He flung his arms over his head as the gun exploded. The shot blasted his hat off and he stumbled. He crashed down on one knee.

He rocketed upright just as fast and lunged to grab the gun away from her. "What the hell do you think you're......?"

She stalked right past him. She didn't even look at him. She jammed her rifle stock into her shoulder firing again and again. The recoil jolted her entire body, but she never removed her cheek from the housing.

Marvin swung around....and froze. Standing right behind him was the most hideous creature he'd laid eyes on. It distantly resembled a buck elk, but instead of antlers, clusters of jagged, gory blades stuck out of its head. Blood stained its coat and head where it trickled down from the blade-antlers. The buck's red eyes glared and sharp claws pawed the air when it rose on its hind legs.

It let out a spine-chilling shriek that stood Marvin's hair on end. His heart quailed, but the woman didn't back down. She planted herself in front of it and emptied her magazine into its chest and up into its head.

The buck flailed its forelimbs and rotated its deadly rack to the skies, but she didn't quit until her gun run dry. She fired the last three slugs into the underside of its jaw and the buck toppled backward. It hit the ground with an earth-shaking thud. It lay still except for a few spasms that soon faded to twitching. Black blood flowed from its mouth

A sick feeling bored into Marvin's insides when he looked at the thing. "What the......What the Holy Hell is that thing?"

The woman spun around to face him. Without missing a beat, she pulled up her skirts and dug a fistful of rifle cartridges out of her pants pocket. She gasped for air, but her hand didn't tremble in the slightest when she started cramming the slugs into her rifle. "I need you to saddle up and come with me right now. Come on. Mount up."

"You hold it right there, lady! I don't know who the hell you think you are, but I'm...."

"I'm your neighbor. I'm Ida Blanchard. I live on the next ranch beyond Granite Ridge." She nodded toward the west. "You're Marvin Powel, aren't you? You just moved out here last October. Sheriff Oliver told me about you."

Marvin squinted at her. He could not for the life of him figure out what she was telling him or how she could act so calm and collected with that.....that thing lying there.

He struggled to put the pieces together. "You're.... you're my neighbor? Why didn't you come over sooner? I've been here six months and I never laid eyes on you."

She cranked down her lever again and her sharp eye checked that the round loaded into the chamber. "Some of us have ranches to run. We don't have time to go riding over creation making social calls. Now are you going to come with me or are you gonna stand here while those things take over your whole ranch?"

"My whole.... what the hell are you talking about? What is that thing? How did it.....?" He floundered to put his thoughts into words. "That thing would have killed me if you didn't.....How did you know that thing was behind me?"

She lowered her hand so her rifle hung next to her thigh at the end of her arm. She straightened up and leveled him with an unflinching gaze. "I'll explain everything if you come with me. We don't have much time."

He scanned her up and down. The more time he spent around her, the more unaccountable she seemed. He didn't know how to reconcile her obvious femininity with what she just did.

"Well....." he stammered, "what are you doing riding around dressed like *that*? What are you...?"

She waited for him to finish, but when he didn't come up with any other intelligible question, her expression softened. "My husband died and I had to take over the ranch. I had to ride and shoot and do everything he used to do, so I started wearing his pants and chaps under my dress. It seemed like the best thing to do at the time."

"Well.....why don't you ride side-saddle like a woman? What are you doing galloping around in that....?" His eyes dipped to her dress again.

"I didn't have a side-saddle or the money to buy one. All I had was my husband's old saddle, so that's what I've been using ever since. Can we go now?"

Marvin slumped. He got on his horse. Ida mounted, too, and Marvin followed her away toward the west.

# Chapter 3

Marvin and Ida sat in their saddles and stared down at the bubble. It hadn't moved since Ida left it. It still occupied the same valley where it appeared this morning. She could still see what used to be her own cattle fighting the elk inside. Bodies littered the grass inside the bubble, but quite a few of the animals were still alive—if she could call them alive at all.

The cattle who were outside the bubble when it first appeared had retreated farther down the valley. They kept well away from the noise and commotion. Ida didn't mind leaving them there. They would be safe there as long as the bubble didn't move or grow.

Ida didn't see her old rifle anywhere. It must still be inside flying around shooting at everything. Then again, it would have run out of bullets long before now.

While she and Marvin gazed at the strange phenomenon, the bluebird rocketed out of the bubble heading for a stand of cottonwoods by the stream. On its way to the branches, it spotted an ordinary badger going about its business nearby.

The badger didn't notice the bluebird at first. It snuffled in the dirt digging a burrow in the tree roots. The bluebird veered and attacked the badger screeching and squealing like a banshee.

The bird stabbed its elongated beak into the badger's shoulder. The badger rounded on the bird with an enraged bellow. It jerked its dust-strew head out of the ground and lunged for the bird.

The bluebird dodged once and barreled in for another assault. The badger checked its trajectory and dove a second time. In half an instant, it snatched the bird out of the air and snapped it in half. It crunched the bluebird in its jaws, shook its head with an angry snort, and spat the bird into the dust before the badger went back to what it was doing.

"So that's what happened," she told Marvin. "I went back to my house to fetch a fresh horse to go get you. While I was saddling up, I saw that buck crossing the draw behind my barn. He was headed for your place and I saw him again on the way across the ridge.

I knew I had to intercept him before he got near your place, but he was too far away to reach, so I went straight to your place instead. I'm sorry I scared you but......"

"It looks like onyx."

Something in his tone made Ida look over. Marvin muttered under his breath like he was talking to himself. He stared at the bubble with a blank, unseeing expression on his face. His features registered none of the horror or disgust he showed when he first saw the buck.

Ida snapped her fingers in front of his face. "Marvin! Stop looking at it. Marvin!"

He jolted backward and whirled around to stare at her. "Huh? Oh, right. Well, what are we gonna do about it?"

"What *can* we do? It isn't as though we can go down there and pop the bubble."

Marvin frowned. "I suppose not."

"What do you suggest? We can't just let it stay here."

"Why not?" Marvin asked. "Whatever harm it *can* do, it's already done. It isn't moving or eating anything else. It looks....." He gazed at it again. "It looks harmless."

"Harmless!" Ida checked herself. "Other animals might go into it and then come out of it changed. It might not be moving now but it could move later. It appeared out of nowhere. It could blink out and appear somewhere else. It might appear in the middle of a city and then think what disasters it would cause."

"Well, what do *you* say we should do about it. I don't see that we can do anything."

"We have to do something. For a start, it's in the middle of my ranch. I can't just leave it here. This valley is the only route between my best grazing areas."

Marvin rubbed his chin. His eyes kept glazing over when he looked at the bubble, but each time, he managed to haul himself back to awareness. "I'll be honest with you. I don't know what to do about it. I never heard of anything like this before."

"I don't think anyone has," Ida admitted. "I can't think of anything that would explain it."

"I suppose, if neither of us knows what to do about it, we could ask someone who does."

"Like who?" Ida asked. "If no one has ever dealt with this before, then no one knows *how* to deal with it. We could ask Sheriff Oliver.... or Samson Phillips, the schoolteacher, but I don't think either of them knows anything about this, either. I don't think anyone does."

Marvin shrugged. "We could ask Reverend Sherman."

Ida almost laughed at the thought, but she stopped herself. When she turned back to look at the bubble, she understood what Marvin meant. If no one had ever dealt with something like this, then maybe Reverend Sherman *was* the right person to ask.

Marvin reined his horse around. Without a word, Ida fell in next to him, but they didn't canter off to town. There didn't seem to be much need to hurry anymore. When they reached the hilltop, she looked back again. The bubble was still there in exactly the same place.

She was starting to get used to the sight of it. It didn't terrify her the way it did before. Now she hated it. She hated it for stealing her cattle and turning them into monsters. She hated it for killing her horse and dozens of other animals. She hated it for taking the beauty of the bluebird and the bumblebee and the stag and turning them into something horrible.

She would destroy the bubble if she could, but how? She didn't dare go near it. Where did it come from? What was its curious power to turn everything it touched evil and murderous?

She and Marvin didn't speak until their horses ambled into the dusty streets of Ballantyne. Marvin nodded toward the nearest saloon. "Let's check in there."

Ida nodded. "It's never too early for Reverend Sherman to be in his office."

They tethered their horses to the hitching post. Laughter, the clink of glasses, and the jingle of coins came from inside the saloon even though the morning wasn't half over. Ida met Marvin at his house just after seven o'clock and they couldn't have been gone more than an hour since then.

Ida caught Marvin checking her appearance when she climbed onto the wooden sidewalk. Her dress fell over her pants and chaps, but it didn't hide her boots. She took her rifle from her saddle when she left her horse and she didn't remove her hat.

She made no effort at all to make herself look more appropriately female, but no one in town noticed. No one looked sideways at her when she rode into town astride her horse like a man. Everyone in Ballantyne already knew about her. Only Marvin found her behavior strange because he didn't know her.

A bunch of half-drunk cattle punchers slouched at the bar and hunched over the gambling tables. Three men sat around a huge stack of bills, coins, and trinkets while the dealer passed out cards for the next hand.

Slim, the bartender, and Matilda, the thick-set madame, served customers behind the bar. Sadie, the working girl, reclined against the bar with half her chest hanging out of her over-tight bodice. She fanned herself with a huge ostrich-feather fan and laughed too loudly at every weak joke the cowhands made to her.

When Marvin and Ida walked in, Farley, the foreman from the Four-Leafed Clover Ranch, leaned in to whisper something to Sadie. He tipped too far and fell full-length against her. She pulled away and he slid to the floor where he crashed onto his face.

"How ya doin', Farley?" Matilda called over without stopping work.

Farley didn't move. He lay where he fell and didn't get up. Sadie laughed. "He's just fine. He couldn't be better."

Laughter erupted. No one noticed Marvin or Ida. Marvin nudged her and nodded toward a corner of the saloon. In the very back corner, a tall, skeletal man in a black suit sat ramrod erect at an isolated table. He faced the corner where he wouldn't have to see any of the sordid doings going on in the rest of the establishment.

The moment Ida laid eyes on him, he raised a tumbler of whiskey to his lips, tossed back a double portion, and replaced the glass in front of him. The full bottle waited at his elbow.

Marvin and Ida made their way through the gambling tables to the spot. They halted where the lonely drinker couldn't fail to see them. "Mornin', Reverend Sherman, Sir," Marvin greeted him. "Good to see you up so early."

"I'm always up early." The Reverend's voice wavered slightly. It seemed to whisper from beyond the grave.

He picked up the whiskey bottle, poured himself another helping, and drank it down. Marvin and Ida exchanged glances. Maybe consulting him about the bubble wasn't the greatest idea after all, but what other option was there?

"You should slow down some," Marvin ventured. "You'll damage yourself drinking like that so early in the morning. It isn't even nine o'clock yet."

Reverend Sherman served himself another half-tumbler of whiskey. A few strands of dust-grey hair clung to his bald dome of a head. He looked more like an undertaker than any preacher Ida ever met.... or maybe he was already a ghost. Ida wouldn't be surprised. Maybe he died a long time ago and just kept haunting this table for lack of anything better to do.

He raised his glass in salute to nobody. "I'm solving the world's problems. A man has to wake up early to do that."

"Maybe you can solve a problem for us," Ida chimed in. "We don't know anyone else who might be able to help."

"Add it to my docket and I will consider it in due course."

"We need it solved now," Ida persisted. "It's some otherworldly force beyond anything we've ever seen before. It came from.... well, it looks like it came from Hell."

"I never deal with business like that." Reverend Sherman poured his next drink without spilling a drop. "You'll have to take anything of that kind to a higher authority."

"But you're a preacher," Ida countered. "Aren't you supposed to shepherd your flock through trials and confrontations with the forces of evil?"

"I take no responsibility for my flock," he husked. "Their immortal souls are their own business."

Marvin and Ida looked at each other again. Marvin pursed his lips and his eyes sparked. "The last I heard, you were drawing a stipend from the good people of this town to support you in exchange for acting as their spiritual leader and religious advisor. If you don't do your job when it's called for, the people of Ballantyne might decide to remove you from office. Then you wouldn't be bringing in the money for all this whiskey you spend your days drinking. Did you ever think of that?"

Apparently Reverend Sherman already *had* thought of it. He poured himself another drink with exaggerated care and his tone didn't flutter in the slightest. "Doing my job is not called for.... or I should rather say that I *am* doing my job by spending my days drinking all this whiskey. This is the job the good people of Ballantyne call me to do and I'm doing it." He tossed back another shot. "I don't hear anyone besides you objecting to my execution of my duties."

Ida cringed. He was right. Ida had lived outside Ballantyne for almost ten years. As far as she knew, Reverend Sherman sat at this table drinking six days out of the week. He only left it to go home to sleep in the evenings and to hold his church services on Sundays. Other than that, this was what the people of Ballantyne paid him to do and no one objected until today.

When she looked at Marvin one more time, she read the same question in his eyes. Reverend Sherman wouldn't or couldn't help them with the bubble—if there was anything anyone could do about it. What could they do instead? Who could they talk to about it?

In answer to her thoughts, loud boot clomps vibrated the floor as another person entered the saloon. Ida glanced over her shoulder and her heart leaped when Sheriff Oliver strode in.

She spun away and hurried over to him. "Sheriff! Thank goodness you're here. You're just the person I was hoping to run into."

He scanned her up and down. "Good morning to you, too, Mrs. Blanchard. What can I do for you?"

He swaggered to the bar, stepped over Farley's insensible form, and leaned one elbow next to Sadie. He cocked his hat back on his head and shot Sadie a rakish grin. She blushed, batted her eyelashes, and fluttered her fan in return.

Ida faltered. She couldn't compete with Sadie for the Sheriff's attention. He was a young, single man and a very good-looking one. The younger girls in town fainted when he walked down the street.

Ida wasn't one of those and he had a reputation for being more interested in them than in hunting down anything unpleasant or dangerous. How could she explain the bubble to him? He would ignore it and he would ignore her.

To her relief, Marvin marched over and rooted himself to the floor at Ida's side. "There's something unusual going on out at Granite Ridge. It's threatening the whole area. We need help to deal with it before it spreads."

The Sheriff actually stopped leering at Sadie long enough to face Marvin. "What is it?"

Marvin hesitated, too, and Ida's heart sank. How could anyone explain the bubble to someone who hadn't seen it themselves? Neither Ida nor Marvin could explain it even to themselves, much less anyone else.

Ida could just hear the wheels turning in Marvin's head. Sheriff Oliver wouldn't ride nine miles over rough country to Granite Ridge to see something no one had ever seen before. What could Marvin and Ida actually say to convince him—that they wanted him to spend the day investigating a giant bubble?

Just then, Matilda waddled over behind the bar. She halted across from them. "What'll you have, Sheriff?"

He turned his back on Marvin to answer her. At that moment, a thunderous boom echoed through town. A powerful concussion blasted out the saloon windows and the impact hurled everyone off their feet.

Ida cartwheeled into Marvin and they both pitched across the nearest gambling table. The whole thing collapsed under their weight and they hit the ground hard. Ida scrambled to see what was going on and her blood ran cold when she beheld the glistening sides of the bubble filling Main Street from one row of buildings to the other.

# Chapter 4

**M**arvin clambered to his feet. His boot heels crunched in a carpet of broken glass. Ida tripped over one of the gamblers when she tried to stand up. She stumbled into Marvin and he caught her to steady her.

His throat tightened when he saw the bubble's margin right outside the saloon window. Through its watery mirror, he could see people and horses and debris caught inside.

The people had changed into grinning devils. Their glowing red eyes narrowed to slits and their mouths leered in fang-encrusted maws too wide for their misshapen heads. Their jaws, cheekbones, and skulls had distorted out of all proportion and their limbs and bodies bent at grotesque angles.

If the scene in the valley made Marvin's sick, the one outside the saloon struck terror into his heart. The people—if they were still people at all—loped along Main Street and beset animals, wagons, and other people in murderous attacks. They would have torn each other limb from limb if their would-be victims didn't fight back with equal ferocity.

Wagons, carts, wheelbarrows, and even hand tools caught the bubble's infection, too. Wagons barreled down Main Street. They teetered right and left at their own whim trying to mow down anything in range. A hatchet somersaulted past the saloon and smashed its head into a wagon careening across its path.

In half a second, the hatchet set to work hacking the wagon to pieces with no one holding its handle. The wagon whirled around to return the assault. It raised its tongue and swatted at the hatchet. It pelted the hatchet away and the tool twirled thirty yards before it stopped in mid-air, hesitated a moment, and then rocketed away somewhere else.

A little girl in a checked gingham dress ran past the saloon. Marvin watched in horror as she spotted a dog turned into a hound from Hell itself. The dog stood in the middle of a hen coop he had torn his way into.

The dog dove right and left snapping at the hens who pummeled him from all directions. They screeched in rage while they ripped into him with their claws, pecked him with their beaks, and beat him with their wings.

The girl ran straight to the breach in the fence. She ducked inside, grabbed the dog, and sank her enormous fangs into his body. The dog roared in pain and tried to thrash his way out of her grip.

Marvin couldn't watch. He turned away. Ida had her head turned aside, too, and she looked ill. Everyone else in the saloon gaped at the bubble in shock.

"What the.....?" Sheriff Oliver rasped. "That isn't....it isn't possible."

"That's what we came to tell you about," Marvin told him. "It appeared on Ida's ranch this morning. Now it's here."

"We have to....." The Sheriff lunged for the door.

Marvin dove into his path and grabbed the young man by the shoulders. He grappled Sheriff Oliver back to the bar. "You are NOT going out there! Don't you see what will happen to you the minute you step inside the bubble? No one is safe as long as it's out there."

As if his words worked some magic spell, Farley heaved off the floor, coughed once, and lurched to the door. Before anyone could stop him, he teetered outside and walked straight into the bubble.

The instant he crossed the margin, he changed. He transformed into a monster and attacked the nearest living thing to him, which happened to be a rabbit hopping across Main Street.

Farley's eyes stretched into slits and he trained his murderous gaze on the rabbit. He broke into a gallop on twisted, gangly legs, but the devil rabbit saw him coming. The rabbit swiveled in its tracks. Its front fangs stuck out of its mouth in long, grinning spikes.

It gathered itself into a ball of jagged spines and launched at Farley. It hit him in the head and the two monsters laid into each other with blood-curdling shrieks.

Marvin didn't want to see what happened next. He hauled his eyes away and faced Sheriff Oliver again. "We have to do something. We have to find a way to stop it."

"How?" the Sheriff croaked. "We can't even get out of the building."

"We can get out," Ida countered. "There's the back stairs from Sadie's apartment."

"How would *you* know about that?" Sadie gave a cruel laugh and leered at the Sheriff, but no one paid any attention to her.

Ida turned to Matilda. "Do you have any weapons in this place?"

"Slim has his shotgun behind the bar," the big madam told her.

Ida shook her head. "That isn't enough. We need guns—a lot of 'em."

"What for?" Sheriff Oliver asked. "We can't shoot the bubble."

"We aren't going to shoot the bubble," Ida replied with condescending slowness. "We have to defend ourselves from any of those people or animals who escapes the bubble. Once they go inside it, they change. If they ever leave it, they stay that way....." She nodded toward the monsters warring across Main Street.

"How do you know so much about it?" Matilda asked.

"That's the reason we came to town this morning," Ida replied. "That bubble appeared on my ranch this morning. An elk stag escaped and almost killed Marvin, but I shot him and he died. Bullets work on those things."

A tense silence fell over the saloon. Everyone turned to stare through the destroyed windows—everyone except Marvin and Ida. Marvin had seen enough of that for one lifetime. He wouldn't look again unless he absolutely had to.

At long last, Matilda cleared her throat. "Right. Well, we're gonna need some weapons, won't we? Sadie, darlin', you go up to my room and bring down every rifle, shotgun, and pistol you can lay your hands on. Slim, you go with her and bring down the ammo."

"But Matilda...." Sadie began.

"No buts!" Matilda snapped. "Get moving. I don't want to be in here if that thing expands and decides to take us with it."

She shot Sadie a look that left no room for argument. Sadie rolled her eyes and slouched out of the room. Slim followed her. A moment later, Marvin heard them climbing the stairs.

Matilda turned back to Ida. "What else can you tell us about that thing? Is there any way to get rid of it?"

Ida glanced behind her and Marvin followed her gaze. Reverend Sherman still sat at the same table. He raised his glass to his lips. He was sipping at it now instead of slamming the whiskey. Did that mean he was well-oiled? He didn't appear to be aware of the disaster unfolding outside.

Ida looked up at Marvin and her eyes spoke volumes to him. "What do you think we ought to do with him? Do you think we should try to reason with him again?"

Marvin shrugged. "I don't think it will do any good, but we can give it a try. One thing I do know. We can't leave him here."

Ida nodded and sighed. "Go talk to him, will you? It can't hurt anything."

Marvin lowered his voice to a whisper only she could hear. "I don't hold out much hope for him.... or us, for that matter. You stay here and get the weapons handed out. Scout the escape route and be ready to move when I come back with him or without him."

"You got it."

Ida turned away and Marvin strode over to Reverend Sherman's table. He didn't relish this project one bit. He knew he couldn't leave Reverend Sherman to a grisly fate, but in that moment, Marvin wrestled with a serious temptation to do exactly that.

He halted in front of the preacher's place. He stared down at the man while Reverend Sherman raised his tumbler again. The gnarled, bony hands didn't tremble. The milky eyes stared straight ahead What would Reverend Sherman turn into if the bubble claimed him? Would he change at all? Maybe Reverend Sherman already *was* a fiend from Hell.

"We're getting out of here, Reverend," Marvin began. "You might want to come with us."

Reverend Sherman looked up at him, but Marvin wasn't sure if Reverend Sherman recognized him or understood those words. "Come with you? Where to?"

"Away from the bubble." Marvin waved toward the window. "You can't stay here. It isn't safe. One of those things might come after you."

Reverend Sherman craned his lizardy neck around and looked toward the window. For the first time, his gaze rested on the bubble. Marvin studied the man for any trace of.... What was Marvin looking for—recognition? Had Reverend Sherman seen the bubble before? How could he? How could anyone have ever seen anything like this before?

Reverend Sherman's expression didn't flinch. No light of recognition came alive in his blurry eyes. Neither did Reverend Sherman register any of the disgust or horror the others felt. He didn't appear to see anything out of the ordinary in the scene outside.

Reverend Sherman got to his feet. He scooted his chair back with deliberate care. The wooden legs screeched on the floor. He drained the last of his drink and tugged his jacket straight. "I'm ready to go."

Marvin didn't budge. "Well?"

"Well what?"

"Don't you have anything to say about that?" Marvin stabbed his finger toward the broken window. "Don't you have anything to say about what we should do about it?"

Reverend Sherman twisted his neck to peer over his shoulder. He strained his eyes toward the bubble as though struggling to see what Marvin was talking about. "What do you mean?"

"Are you seriously telling me you don't see that? Are you telling me you don't see the townspeople changed into monsters? Christ, man, they're tearing each other apart out there!"

Reverend Sherman scrutinized the scene on Main Street with all his concentration. "It looks the same to me."

Marvin gaped at him. The same? How could it be the same? Against his will, Marvin glanced beyond Reverend Sherman's shoulder to the street. He caught a fleeting glimpse of three housewives in their aprons and work dresses. He recognized them from the Ladies' Aid Society. They ran a fundraising bake stall on the lawn outside the church after services every Sunday.

Now, they surrounded an old man who lay prostrate on the ground while the three women pounded him with shovels, sledgehammers, and random sticks of wood. The old man clutched something in his hands, but Marvin forced himself to look away before he recognized it.

He rounded on Reverend Sherman, who gazed at him with no expression at all. For the first time, Marvin thought he understood what the preacher was trying to say in his drunken way. "You say....it looks the same."

"It's always this way," Reverend Sherman murmured. "It never changes."

Marvin's head spun trying to understand. "Are you saying you've seen this before?"

Reverend Sherman shrugged. "It's always like this. It never changes."

"Is there any way to stop it? Isn't there any way to....to change it back?"

"It will never stop. It always has been this way and it always will. They'll never change."

Marvin's blood ran cold. What would it take to turn a man of God into Reverend Sherman? What poison must have infected his mind that he saw that horror all the time? No wonder he drank so much.

Just then, Ida came over to them. "What's going on? What did you find out?"

Marvin glanced at her once. He couldn't tell her what Reverend Sherman said. He couldn't tell Ida that Reverend Sherman said it was hopeless. If Reverend Sherman was right, the bubble would grow and expand until it covered the whole world. If Reverend Sherman was right, it already had.

"He doesn't know anything."

"The weapons are all loaded and passed out—all but yours, Marvin." She furrowed her brow at the preacher. "I don't think he'll be much good to us."

Marvin turned away. "Let's move out."

She returned to the group at the bar. Besides Sheriff Oliver, Matilda, Slim, and Sadie, two of the former gamblers remained. Marvin didn't know them and none of the others were here. They must have run off like Farley.

Marvin took hold of Reverend Sherman's arm. "Come on. You're coming with us."

Reverend Sherman followed his directions. Ida shoved two shotguns and a rifle into Marvin's hands. He checked each one to make sure the magazines were full—not that he doubted Ida. She wouldn't hand him a gun that wasn't ready to shoot.

He checked the group one more time while he draped the two shotgun straps over his torso. The Sheriff looked rattled and almost ready to cry. Fantastic. That was just what Marvin needed right now. He put more faith in Slim, Matilda, and Sadie. Each one handled their weapons with confident ease.

The two gamblers were a different story. They kept glancing toward the bubble and getting hypnotized by it. Marvin made a note to himself not to count on them too much, either.

No one paid any attention to Reverend Sherman. The party gathered by the bar and Marvin, Ida, Sadie, Matilda, Slim, and Sheriff Oliver closed in a circle. When the lead started flying, Marvin would have these five—no one else.

"The way out goes up the stairs, through Sadie's apartment, down the back hall to the back stairs, and down to the alley," Ida began. "Assuming none of those things comes into the saloon, we should be clear until we get outside."

"And after we get outside?" Matilda asked.

"Then it's all on," Ida replied. "I think we can assume those things are leaving the bubble and running wild all over town. They'll be attacking healthy people the way that bird attacked the badger."

"What badger?" Sadie asked.

"Never mind," Ida corrected. "Marvin and I have seen this before. Infected creatures leave the bubble and attack healthy creatures."

"What do we do then?" Sheriff Oliver asked.

"Then we shoot. Don't hesitate and shoot to kill. It doesn't matter if it's someone you know. They aren't the same. They'll kill you if they can. Your only hope is to kill them first."

Matilda and Slim nodded. Sheriff Oliver and Sadie weren't so certain, but Marvin no longer cared. If these people couldn't shoot to save their own lives, he couldn't put himself or the others at risk to help them.

He cast one more appraising look at the faces around him. The longer he stood here, the more certain he became of just exactly who he could count on and who would fall by the wayside.

He raised his rifle and jacked down the lever. "Let's move."

# Chapter 5

I da whirled away and hustled to the end of the bar. She ducked behind the curtain that separated the saloon from the back room. She paused there to look back. Matilda, Sadie, and Slim followed right behind her ready to make a break for freedom.

Marvin came next leading Reverend Sherman by the elbow. The preacher shuffled after him like a mindless child. Sheriff Oliver brought up the rear with the two gamblers.

They closed behind the rest of the group and Ida lifted the curtain to leave the saloon. She looked over her shoulder to make sure that everyone kept up. At that moment, the bubble thumped outward with a devastating bang. The margin smashed into the saloon and tore the front walls out. The bubble expanded into the room where the party just stood.

In a split second, it enveloped the two gamblers. The noise alerted Marvin. He flung Reverend Sherman out of the way. Marvin barely caught Sheriff Oliver in time to yank the young man clear.

The two gamblers changed in a blink. They twisted into hideous shapes and their mouths widened into grinning pits. They rotated toward each other, shrieked in rising frenzy, and then launched out of the bubble to attack the fleeing party.

Marvin whipped around still struggling to pull Sheriff Oliver out of their path. Marvin swung his rifle around, but he was too close to the gamblers. They flew at him and Sheriff Oliver and pounced before either man could get their weapons into position.

One fiend hit Sheriff Oliver and the other landed on Marvin. Its weight knocked him backward and he felt himself falling. The thing lunged for his face. A mouth full of fangs rushed at his eyes.

Lightning quick, he shoved his rifle into the creature's jaws and the fangs clamped around the metal. A tooth sliced Marvin's finger. Pain fired through him and fueled him to superhuman strength.

He needed every ounce of it to hold the thing off. The creature's claws clenched through his clothes and into his sides. The jaws snapped the rifle in half as though it wasn't there and the monster made another rush at Marvin's head. He didn't have time to act.

At that moment, someone stuck a gun in his face. The barrel stabbed into the thing's forehead and the gun exploded inches from Marvin's eyes. The impact stunned him and he felt the blessed relief of the demon ripping off him.

Strong hands grabbed him and hauled him to his feet. "Get up, Marvin! Hurry!"

Ida dragged him still reeling to the curtain. The stars didn't leave his brain until he stumbled into the back room, where everyone paused to gather their wits.

Ida eased in close to Marvin and squeezed his arm. "You okay?"

He nodded. He never doubted for a second that she was the one who shot that thing and saved his life.... again. She grabbed the strap of one of his shotguns and looped it over his head. She checked the chamber like a real soldier and pushed the gun into his grasp. "Here. Take it."

His fingers closed around the cold steel. She tapped him again. "Let's go—up the stairs, through the apartment, and down the hall."

The group caught Marvin in its current. Slim and Sadie flanked him with Ida and Matilda in front. If the others were behind him, Marvin didn't see them. He kept Ida in sight. She consumed his whole attention. She would get them out of here. She had to.

The group climbed the stairs and rushed through an apartment decked out with red gauze draped around the bed. Ida led the way into the hall and to another door at its far end.

She stopped there, eased the door back, and peeked through. She shut it and rounded on the party. "Once we get outside, we head for the church. The vestry is adjacent to the livery stable. We can get horses there."

"We don't know if the church or the livery stable aren't inside the bubble," Sheriff Oliver pointed out.

"If they are, we move on. We'll push on for the school. It's far enough out of town that the bubble probably hasn't extended that far."

"We won't be able to get horses there," Sadie remarked.

"The Lytle farm isn't far away from the school," Slim suggested. "Max Lytle will have horses."

Ida nodded. "Good. We'll gather at the school. If we get separated, head for the school. We'll take shelter there before we push on for the Lytle farm. Is everyone clear on the plan?"

Everyone nodded. Sheriff Oliver, Ida, and Matilda checked their weapons for the hundredth time. Marvin distinctly saw Sadie move closer to Ida.

Ida checked each person one after another. Then she nodded again. "Here we go."

She peeked again through a crack in the door. Then she flung it all the way open, whipped her rifle to her shoulder, and charged for the stairs. She dashed down them two at a time sweeping her gun barrel everywhere.

Marvin did the same thing. Monsters of various species battled all around them, but they were all too occupied with their own brand of murderous mayhem to bother the friends.

Ida sprang to the ground and dashed east, away from the bubble. Marvin made it to the alley. The bubble's dark edge cut between two buildings not far away. Disfigured shapes darted back and forth beyond the shadowy rim, but he didn't try to distinguish them. They were lost in there, whatever they were.

He jerked his gun in all directions to make sure none of those things came near him. The group wheeled and raced down the alley making for open country beyond the houses, stores, and businesses of Main Street. The empty land out there called Marvin to get as far away from town as possible.

Ida streaked for the church. The alley ended past the dry goods store and she paused at the corner to check the way forward. Matilda and Sadie crowded in behind her. "What do you see out there?" Sadie whispered. "Where's the bubble? How far out is it?"

"The church is gone, but….."

"It's always like this," Reverend Sherman muttered.

Ida ignored him. "The livery stable is okay, though. We should head for that."

"Are you sure it isn't too close to the bubble?" Sadie peeped. "I don't want to get too near it."

"I don't, either." Ida turned around and her eyes found everyone in the group. Her gaze offered a breath of life to Marvin. "I'll admit it's a risk, but I think we should chance it. We can get horses there. We'll get farther away from town quicker. If we go for the school instead, we'll be covering almost two miles on foot. What do you all think?"

The others exchanged glances. "I'm with Ida," Matilda said finally. "The sooner we get on horseback, the better."

Sadie gulped. "All right. If you both think it's best, I'll go, too."

"What about you, Marvin?" Ida asked. "Are you with us?"

"You know I'm with you, darlin'," he replied. "I'm with you all the way."

She burst into a brilliant grin and color flushed her cheeks. She really was beautiful.

Sheriff Oliver squinted around the corner. "How are we gonna do this? The bubble looks like it's between the jail and the dry goods store. We'll only be in sight of it for a few stretches of ground. Marvin and I, Matilda, Slim, and Ida—we should travel on the right. We'll put ourselves between the bubble and Sadie and Reverend Sherman. Agreed?"

"Good idea," Ida replied. "Everybody okay with that?"

Everyone nodded again. Ida, Marvin, Sheriff Oliver, Slim, and Matilda rotated into position. Sadie steered Reverend Sherman to the inside where the others could protect them.

Ida made one last check on everyone and stormed into the open. The five shooters swiveled their guns toward the bubble. Marvin searched all around him for the slightest hint of movement. He didn't bother looking inside the bubble. He only cared about what might be outside it.

The party migrated in a line toward the livery stable. The dry goods store passed and Marvin glanced down another alley toward Main Street. The bubble cut between the buildings with the storefronts blasted out and destroyed. The buildings yawned open in shattered wreckage.

The next minute, the jail cut off his view. Out of the corner of his eye, he saw Ida and Sheriff Oliver steering Slim and Matilda around a water trough. The stable was a hundred yards away at the most. Just a few more minutes and the party would be inside it.

The jail swiveled past his eyes and he lost sight of the bubble. His spirits lifted. This might actually work. The group would mount up and ride far, far away from the bubble and all its horrors.

Sheriff Oliver touched Marvin's elbow. He glanced over expecting another obstacle in his path. A few yards away, Ida and Matilda broke away from the group to make their last dash to safety.

At that moment, a piercing screech startled Marvin out of his head. Everyone spun around in time to see a monstrous bull thunder out of nowhere. Lightning sparked from jagged, blade-like horns and licks of flame ignited every time his hooves touched the ground.

He charged the group and, before anyone could move, he snatched Sadie by her bodice laces. He yanked her clean off her feet and hauled her backward toward the wasteland outside of town.

Sadie struggled against his teeth. She wrenched herself around and flung out her arms. Her screams stabbed into Marvin's brain. Sadie scrambled to catch hold of something, anything. Reverend Sherman surprised everyone by springing to life as though he'd been shot.

He dove for Sadie and his lifeless fingers cinched around both her wrists. His fists thumped against her knuckles as the bull hauled her away with another fearsome tug. She shrieked to wake the dead. Reverend Sherman dug in his heels and leaned almost over backward fighting to hold onto her.

The bull gave one more horrendous jerk and pulled Reverend Sherman off his feet, too. The preacher slammed to the ground still grappling to maintain his hold on Sadie, but it was no good. His fall dislodged his hands.

The bull yanked Sadie away. She screamed again. Marvin charged for the bull, but when he sighted down his weapon for the creature's head, he remembered he was holding a shotgun instead of a rifle. He couldn't shoot without hitting Sadie, too.

Ida barged up next to Marvin, her face transfigured in fury. "Sadie!"

"Help me, Ida!" Sadie shrieked. "Ida, don't leave me! Help me!"

"Hold on, Sadie!" Ida roared. "Hold on!"

Those words hardly left her lips when the bull wheeled and galloped away. He raised his proud head dangling Sadie by the back of her dress. She flopped with every bouncing step and her continuous screeches echoed all over town.

Ida barreled forward to go after them, but Marvin caught her arm. "Stop! Not that way. We have to circle around." He sliced his finger back the way they came, behind the saloon, and toward the courthouse. "We'll split up. Sheriff, you, Slim, and Matilda drive the bull from behind. Ida and I will flank him. I'll take the courthouse and Ida will take the saloon building. Understand?"

Everyone nodded but Ida. She compressed her lips in frustrated defeat. This nightmare was taking its toll on her. Losing Sadie took the wind out of her sails.

Sheriff Oliver, Slim, and Matilda moved off. Marvin squeezed Ida's elbow exactly the way she did after that gambler nearly killed him. "We'll get her back. I promise."

She nodded fast. Her distracted eyes skimmed the area without seeing anything. "I just don't think I can....."

"Yes, you can," he breathed. "Now go off to the saloon building. Flank the bull on the north side. Understand? I'll be right across from you behind the courthouse. We're getting Sadie back. You hear me?"

She nodded again, but her heart wasn't in it. Only his words propelled her forward. He pushed her toward the saloon building. She turned away and hurried to follow his instructions.

He stole one last look at her and then made tracks for the courthouse. The best way to help Ida right now was to get Sadie back. He refused to leave Reverend Sherman behind in the saloon and they wouldn't leave Sadie behind, either. As long as they had one normal person with them, they wouldn't leave anyone behind. Marvin would rather die himself and he knew Ida well enough in a few short hours to know she felt the same way.

He ducked behind the courthouse and took up a position in sight of the bubble's edge. The sheriff and the others would drive the bull through here. The bull would head straight for the bubble. He would present his huge sides to gunfire from both Marvin and Ida. He would go down and drop Sadie. Then the group could take her with them to the livery stable and ride away.

A narrow backstreet separated the courthouse from what was left of the saloon building. Ida slid behind the building and took her place where Marvin could see her. She wedged her rifle against a few splintered boards and sighted into the street waiting for the bull to show himself.

Sadie's screams came closer by the second. Her voice trembled in time to the bull's hoofbeats. He was bringing her straight to them.

The bull wheeled into sight and paused when it saw the bubble. For some reason, the animal turned back. It didn't want to take Sadie into the bubble. Why? The bull rotated back the way it came and came face to face with Sheriff Oliver, Slim, and Matilda.

If Marvin ever doubted Sheriff Oliver's resolve, that doubt evaporated when he saw the sheriff sighting down his weapon. Sheriff Oliver gritted his teeth in grim determination and marched straight for the bull with the others at his side.

The bull lowered his head and a growl rumbled from his huge body. Sheriff Oliver fired. The bullet winged the bull's shoulder. The creature bellowed in rage and tossed its head, but it didn't let go of Sadie.

"Help!" she shrieked. "For God's sake, help me!"

Ida inched closer to the corner. She removed her weapon from the boards and locked it into her shoulder. Marvin copied her ready to blast the bull to kingdom come as soon as he laid eyes on the beast.

Sheriff Oliver fired one more time. This time, he clipped the bull across the foreleg. The bull spun away as if to make a break for the bubble, but instead, he whirled in a complete circle. He dropped Sadie right there and the animal charged the three drivers.

Sadie hit the ground and screeched again. Ida swept out of her hiding place as Sheriff Oliver, Slim, and Matilda all opened up with their rifles. They bombarded the bull with dozens of shots, but the creature didn't go down. He didn't turn aside an inch.

Ida sprang into the street aiming for the monster from behind. Marvin lunged out to join her, but he got there a fraction of a second too late.

Ida fired and the bullet punched the bull in the hindquarters. He made a dive for Sheriff Oliver. The sheriff sidestepped out of the creature's path. He traced his rifle barrel to follow the animal. Sheriff Oliver fired his last two bullets sideways into the animal's chest.

The bull thundered past Sheriff Oliver, but instead of running away or falling down, the bull gave another toss of his grisly head and leaped completely around. He spun back down the street and charged for the bubble.

Ida squinted down her rifle barrel firing again and again, but the bull didn't turn aside. Her bullets glanced off his iron skull, but he kept on plunging straight for her even when she dodged to get out of his way. With one dive, he plunged for her and butted her square in the chest. He propelled her backward and she staggered into the bubble.

Marvin sprang forward to grab her. "Ida, no!" He was too late. The whole thing happened so fast he hardly realized until she tripped over her own feet. Her skirts tangled around her legs and she vanished inside the bubble.

# Chapter 6

T he noise and commotion snuffed out and Ida looked around her, stunned. She knew Ballantyne like the back of her hand. This was a different place, a completely different town. The buildings weren't the same shape or in the same positions. She would recognize if they were.

For a start, the buildings were all enormously tall—much taller than the wooden storefronts and ramshackle houses in Ballantyne. These towered over a street paved in some hard, smooth substance she'd never seen before. It wasn't even cobblestone. It stretched in an unbroken mat from one sidewalk to the other. Only a few cracks and holes marred its flat surface.

The buildings' high fronts bore the unmistakable damage of blasts that exploded them to smithereens. Ida could look through the shattered walls to rooms, hallways, and torn doorways inside. In one of them, a bedstead tilted on its end against the corner.

She stumbled a few paces searching everywhere for some landmark to tell her where she was. She couldn't see the bubble anymore. It was right behind her when the bull knocked her into this queer place. Now it was gone. The street extended behind her with more destroyed buildings lining both flanks.

She staggered farther up the street. She had nowhere to go. She had nothing but the clothes on her back. She didn't even have her rifle anymore. The bull knocked it out of her hands when he butted her.

Muffled booms and rattling gunfire broke the stillness. Other than that, a dull wind moaned between the wrecks all around her. No other sound disturbed the ghostly landscape. Where was everyone? Not a living soul inhabited this landscape.

That wasn't possible, though, was it? Someone must be setting off those explosions and shooting those guns. Did she dare to go near them in the hope of finding someone? What if everyone in this place was a monster like the ones in Ballantyne?

Something strange was going on. None of the animals or monsters from Ballantyne was anywhere nearby. The wagons, guns, tools, and creatures that warred on Main Street weren't here, either. They couldn't be because this wasn't Ballantyne. This was something else—somewhere else.

Piles of trash blocked the gutter. A child's doll rested on top of the stack. Its hair had been partially pulled off and one eye was missing. A metal spoon lay twisted and smashed a few feet away.

She raised her eyes from the spoon and her heart quailed when she surveyed her surroundings one more time. People lived here—at least, they used to. Where were they now? Were they all dead—the victims in this eerie war?

This was definitely a warzone, but the people were long gone. Was this what happened to a town after the monsters finished with it? She wouldn't be surprised.

*She* wasn't a monster, though. She still had regular fingers and her face felt the same. She didn't lose her mind when she stumbled into the bubble. She wasn't running around looking for victims to impale and dismember. Was everything she saw inside the bubble an illusion? That stag wasn't an illusion. It left the bubble and went in a straight line to kill Marvin.

She shuddered, but before she could take another step, a colossal boom shook the ground. It pounded into her very bones, and right in front of her, one of the giant buildings detonated in a cloud of dust and debris. It folded in on itself and collapsed into a heap of rubble.

Ida sprang back from the noise. The rumble of falling rock faded to the patter of stones. She stood stock-still hardly daring to breathe. She stared at where the building used to be. What could do that to one of those giant structures? Wasn't the building already ruined enough without bringing it to the ground?

A lump swelled in her throat. She was trapped here with no way out—not that she much wanted to return to Ballantyne in its current state. She wanted to go home. She wanted.... those people, those people who left the saloon with her. She wanted a few good people around her. Was that too much to ask?

She huddled in on herself fighting off mounting despair. She dared not take another step in case an explosion like that hit her next. She couldn't know if she was moving away from the bubble's margin or toward it. Was there any earthly way of getting back to Ballantyne or was the town lost to her forever?

She gulped down her anguish. She had to think. She had to do something—anything. She looked right and left....and at that moment, something flew at her from behind. She had half a second to recognize Marvin rocketing toward her from out of nowhere. He soared through the air with his arms outstretched.

The next instant, he collided with her in a flying tackle. He hit her hard and they both went down with a brutal thump. She clamped her arms around him for dear life. She was too relieved to see him to think of anything else.

They clutched each other on the cracked pavement. The thought just entered her head that she was holding him close the way she used to hold her husband when someone grasped each of them by the ankle.

Ida glanced down to see Reverend Sherman grabbing her and Marvin. Reverend Sherman's legs vanished behind the bubble's rippling, shadowy edge. The top half of him lay on the solid pavement of this other world and his unwavering eyes drilled into Ida's very soul. His features set in a granite visage of unbending intent.

The next instant, something yanked him backward. An invisible force hauled him out of the bubble and he dragged Marvin and Ida with him.

They skidded past the bubble's rim into the dust and smoke of Ballantyne. Marvin crushed Ida in his arms until they skidded to a halt in front of the courthouse. Sadie, Matilda, Sheriff Oliver, and Slim fell over each other from the effort of dragging all three hostages out of the bubble.

Matilda hopped to her feet. She narrowed her eyes at the bubble and swung her rifle into position aiming for its surface. "We have to get out of here. We're too close to it. Anything could come along and knock one of us back inside."

Sheriff Oliver nodded and dusted off the seat of his pants. "You're right. Let's make tracks for the school. Even the livery stable is too close." He glanced down and caught Ida staring up at him. "Are you two all right? Did any of those things get to you, Ida?"

Ida stared at him. Then she checked the others. They were all perfectly normal. Marvin was okay, too, even after coming inside the bubble to get her. Reverend Sherman looked more alert and attentive than she'd seen him in years.

He bent down and took her hand. He helped her to her feet. She stared at him in amazement. "What did you do, Reverend? How did you save us?"

"It's always like this." His blurry eyes wandered toward the bubble. "It has always been like this and it always will be."

She followed his gaze. Beyond the swirling eddies of color and shadow on the bubble's surface, monstrous forms battled as terribly as ever. Through the dark apparition, she could see the businesses, buildings, and stores of Main Street. She was back in Ballantyne.

"What was it like in there?" Sadie croaked.

"There's no time to talk about that now." Matilda shoved Ida's rifle back into her hands. "If you aren't hurt, Marvin, let's go."

Marvin wasn't hurt. No one was. Sheriff Oliver and Matilda led the way behind the courthouse and onto the open planes. Reverend Sherman walked on his own without being led. He cast backward glances toward Ballantyne and he scanned the surrounding countryside like he understood exactly what was going on.

The farther away from town the group hiked, the fewer monstrous creatures and fiends they saw. The odd demonic bird or insect whizzed by, but they attacked each other or other animals their own size.

The group pressed on through scrub and dry creek beds. The friends kept their guns up ready to shoot at a moment's notice. Ida swept her weapon left and right searching for anything that might come near them.

The schoolhouse rose in sight. Ida could see the Ballantyne courthouse, but not much more of the town itself. The bubble's glistening dome rose over the courthouse spire. It enveloped almost the entire town and hid everything underneath.

Sheriff Oliver opened the schoolhouse door and the group hustled inside. He slammed it behind them. Marvin, Slim, and Reverend Sherman grabbed several desks and even the schoolmaster's lectern. They crammed everything against the door to barricade themselves inside.

Ida raced to the nearest window and aimed her rifle toward the glass, but she couldn't see anything coming after them. All the sordid horrors were trapped in Ballantyne.

Sadie flopped onto the floor in a corner and whimpered. "I'm thirsty. Isn't there anything to eat or drink in this place?"

Reverend Sherman got the water bucket from its place and carried it to her side. He sat down cross-legged next to her and handed her the wooden dipper filled with cool water. "Not to worry, my dear girl. We'll get out of here and go somewhere safe."

Marvin squinted through an east-facing window. "We'll rest here for a little while and then press on to the Lytle farm. We'll get horses and head into the countryside. The bubble isn't moving and it doesn't look like any of those things knows enough to follow us."

"Where will we go?" Slim asked. "If what you said is true and that thing first appeared at Granite Ridge this morning before it came here, then it could leave Ballantyne and reappear anywhere. Nowhere would be safe."

"It appeared on my ranch this morning," Ida replied. "If it did go somewhere else, I don't see it going back to the same place twice. We'd be able to get food and water at my place, too, and I have plenty of guns and ammo."

"What was it like inside that thing?" Sheriff Oliver asked. "Was it as awful as it looks?"

Everyone turned around and stared at Ida. Even Marvin watched her and waited to hear what she would say. She hesitated. What *should* she say? "It was awful, but.....different. I can't explain it."

"What do you mean?" Matilda asked. "Different how?"

Ida shrugged. Here went nothing. "It was completely different. It was a completely different place. It wasn't Ballantyne at all. It was some city, but it was utterly destroyed. It looked like a war happened there—or maybe it already did happen—but it wasn't Ballantyne."

"What about the monsters?" Slim asked. "Did you see them?"

"No. They weren't there. There was nothing." She glanced over at him. "What about you? Did you see *me* through the bubble? Did I turn into a monster?"

The others exchanged glances. None of them answered her. Matilda pinched her lips and looked away. Even Marvin avoided her gaze.

She rounded on him. "Well? Answer me, Marvin. Did I turn into a monster?"

"Yes! You were hideous and you attacked....." He broke off.

Ida gaped at him with her mouth hanging open. She turned into a monster. She read the same truth on all their faces. Marvin glared at her, his features black with fury. Matilda's lips compressed in a tight, white line.

Ida shivered. She didn't want to know what she did inside the bubble. She didn't want to know who or what she attacked while she was standing around that strange city looking at dolls and spoons.

"You don't remember it, do you?" Sadie piped up. "You don't remember being a monster."

"No!" Ida blurted out. "I wasn't a monster. I'm telling you the truth. I was in a completely different city with some kind of stone paving covering the whole street. The buildings were countless stories high and.... there was some kind of battle going on out of sight. I wasn't.... I wasn't a monster. I checked. I had regular hands and my face was the same. I didn't attack anybody! You have to believe me."

"I believe you," Marvin murmured.

An inexpressible wave of gratitude flooded her. She wanted to put her arms around him again. He was the one who saved her. He was the one who came after her and got her the hell out of there.

"If you saw me as a monster, why did you come after me? *You* could have turned into a monster, too."

He shrugged, but before he could say anything, Reverend Sherman spoke up. "It's always like this. It's the same every time. It never changes."

Ida squatted down in front of him. "How did you know? How did you know you could get us out? What do you know about that thing?"

"I don't know anything about it except that it shows something that's already there. The killing, the monstrosity—it's all there. It's there all the time if you only look for it."

"Why the Christ would anybody want to look for it?" Sheriff Oliver snapped.

"Some of us see it all the time." Reverend Sherman looked down at the water bucket. He absently lifted the dipper, poured the water from it back into the bucket, and replaced the dipper before doing it all over again. "Some of us can't help but see it all the time."

"That's because you're a drunken lout with no hope in life," Matilda snarled. "Only you could see it all the time because only you could be hopeless enough to go looking for it."

"How did you know how to get us out?" Ida asked. "You came halfway in. You had your legs still outside the bubble. Did that have something to do with it?"

"I could have come all the way in. I could have traveled a thousand miles inside it to find you and still gotten you out."

"How?" Slim asked.

"By keeping a continuous line between you and the outside. An unbroken line of hearts between you and the.... the other world....it saves you from the darkness."

"Wait a minute." Ida shut her eyes trying to understand him. "You created an unbroken line of people.... all connected to each other. That's how you got us out?"

"Anyone can do it," Reverend Sherman insisted. "It can be anyone as long as their hearts are pure."

Without meaning to, Ida's eyes snapped to Sadie and then to Matilda, Sheriff Oliver, and finally to Slim and Marvin. None of them was what she would call pure. They were anything but—every last living one of them.

Fortunately, no one took offense at her assumption. Matilda started laughing her rolling, cackling laugh. "I hate to break it to you, Reverend, but my heart ain't pure and neither is Sadie's or Slim's. We're just about the farthest thing from pure as a person can be."

"That goes for all of us," Ida murmured.

"If I understand the Reverend right," Marvin put in, "then we should be able to get anyone out of there. All we have to do is make a human chain."

"Your hearts must be pure," Reverend Sherman reminded him. "It won't work if they aren't."

"What do you mean by pure?" Slim asked. "Do you mean without sin?"

"It can't mean that," Matilda added. "Sadie, Sheriff Oliver, you, and I all helped to pull them out and none of us is without sin."

"I don't think he means without sin," Marvin replied. "I think what he means is that we have to sincerely want to save the person from the darkness."

Ida turned back to Reverend Sherman. "Is that right? Is that what you mean by pure of heart?"

He leaned his head back against the wall and half-closed his eyes. "It's always like this. It will never change."

She had to summon all her patience to keep up this vacuous conversation. "How did you know? How did you know you could form the chain and get us out?"

He shut his eyes the rest of the way. "I didn't. I just...went in. I wanted to save you...and Marvin. When Marvin went in to get you, I wanted to do something. I reacted without thinking."

"How do you know about forming a continuous line of hearts, then?" Marvin demanded. "How do we know you aren't just making that shit up to trick us?"

To everyone's surprise, Reverend Sherman actually opened his eyes and beamed up at Marvin. A boyish grin spread over his ghastly features and transformed him from a mummified relic into a vibrant, engaging person. "It's always like this, Marvin. How many times do I have to tell you? I see these things everywhere. That darkness you speak of is everywhere, all the time. There is only one thing that can defeat it and that is a continuous line of pure hearts connected and united through their desire to embrace the light." He giggled like he just made a ridiculous joke. "Everybody knows that." He scanned from one face to the next. "Are you telling me that none of you has seen this before? Are you really telling me you don't know?"

Ida looked around to find the others exchanging uncomfortable glances. He might have a point...of sorts. In a way, he was right. Darkness, killing, hatred—it existed everywhere.

Whatever that strange city was that she saw inside the bubble—darkness, killing, and hatred existed there, too. It was as monstrous and barbaric as the wholesale battle going on in Ballantyne right now—just different. If people became monsters there, they must have been fighting each other on the battlefield she couldn't see.

Sheriff Oliver turned away. He clomped to the western window and cast a fleeting glance toward town. Even from her position on the floor, Ida could see the bubble in the distance. It reflected the sun and shimmered against the sky.

"Let's get out of here," Sheriff Oliver declared. "Let's get to the Lytle farm and get ourselves some horses."

"What about the Lytles?" Slim asked. "If it isn't safe for us this close to town, we should evacuate them. We should warn anyone we can to get away from town."

"I think you mean," Matilda countered, "that if it *is* safe for us this far from town, it will be safe for the Lytles, too. They'll be as safe at their place as they would be at Granite Ridge or anywhere else. As long as they're in no danger from the bubble or the monsters, they can stay where they are."

Slim shrugged, but he didn't answer. "The most important thing," Sheriff Oliver went on, "is to get ourselves to safety. We'll warn the Lytles. If they feel they're in danger, they can come with us."

# Chapter 7

Marvin, Slim, and Sheriff Oliver removed the desks and lectern from the door and Marvin peeked outside. Ida checked her rifle. She had reloaded when the party left Ballantyne, but now her pockets were empty.

She had no idea how much ammo the rest of the party had, but when she spotted Marvin checking his shotgun, she didn't like the look on his face. He didn't look happy at all.

There was no time to worry about that. Sheriff Oliver opened the door and the party marched outside. The sun glared directly overhead and the planes baked in the heat. After a few minutes of not seeing any monsters, Ida gave up pointing her rifle everywhere and slung the strap over her shoulder.

She untied her apron and handed it to Sadie. She helped the girl drape the apron over her bare head, shoulders, and breast. The girl's skimpy dress left her pale skin exposed and prone to burning.

Sadie struggled to return Ida's smile. Ida's heart went out to her, but there was nothing to do but keep going. After more than an hour's walk, they came to the railroad tracks cutting through the empty country. The group followed them until a low farmhouse appeared out of the scrub.

Max and Beatrice Lytle rushed out of their house when the party arrived. A crowd of Lytle children watched from the door as their parents met the strangers coming. "What in the world?" Beatrice exclaimed. "Sheriff, what brings you here? Reverend—my goodness!"

"Sorry to barge in on you like this," Sheriff Oliver replied. "Ballantyne is under siege. We just had to fight our way out of it at the risk of our lives."

"Under siege!" Max boomed. "How do you mean?"

"It's a long story," Marvin told him. "If you don't mind, we need to borrow your horses. If you know what's good for you, you'll evacuate to a safe distance."

"Which is what?" Slim pointed out. "We don't know what a safe distance is or even if there *is* a safe distance."

"It's a manner of speaking," Marvin growled back.

Sheriff Oliver held up his hand for quiet. "We don't know what that thing is or what it will do." He turned back to Max and Beatrice. "Whatever you do, don't go anywhere near town. If you feel you're in danger here, then by all means, evacuate. Otherwise, you might as well stay here. One course is as good as the other as far as I can tell."

Max and Beatrice looked at each other. "How can we decide what to do when we don't know what the danger is?"

"I'm sorry," Sheriff Oliver told them. "I wish I could explain it better, but I don't know what the danger is myself. We just walked from town and we barely made it out. We're heading to the Blanchard place on Granite Ridge. You're both welcome to come with us and bring your children."

"What about my stock?" Max waved toward the barn. "I've got twenty cows and seven newborn calves and that's saying nothing about my sheep and goats. If I go with you, I suppose I'll have to leave 'em all behind."

"I'm afraid so," Sheriff Oliver replied.

Max pursed his lips. He checked his wife and then his children. "I suppose we'll be staying put, then."

Sheriff Oliver shrugged. "I don't blame you and I don't say it won't be the best course in the end, anyway. Now, do you mind if we borrow a few of your horses? We can double up to save you from letting us take too many."

"Take as many as you want." He started leading the friends toward the barn.

Sheriff Oliver, Slim, and Matilda went with him. Beatrice darted in and squeezed Matilda's arm. "I'll get you some food. I'll meet you there."

She raced for the house and shooed her children inside. Reverend Sherman started after the others. Marvin moved in and waved Ida to join him. "Come on, Ida. You'll be home in no time."

Ida didn't budge. She watched Max taking Sheriff Oliver and Slim into the barn. She couldn't go in there. She couldn't ride away.

Marvin swiveled around in front of her and cut off her view of the others. "What's wrong?" he whispered in her face. "What's the problem? Let's go. Let's get out of here. We're going back to Granite Ridge. Isn't that what you wanted?"

Her eyes snapped to his face. If she could explain to anyone, she could tell him. "I can't, Marvin!" Her voice cracked with buried emotion. "I can't leave. I have to go back to Ballantyne. There has to be a way to break the bubble. Reverend Sherman said a continuous line of pure hearts can bring back the light."

He snorted, but he kept his voice low to match hers. "You want to bank your life on what Reverend Sherman says? You'll excuse me if I don't call that a safe bet."

"It's the only way to save the town. I have to try. We can't just ride away and save ourselves with that thing hanging over our town—I mean, *I* can't. It could stay there forever. It could spread to the whole state for all we know. If there's a way to break it, we have to try it. *I* have to try it."

He pinched his lips and looked over his shoulder. Max was leading a horse out of the barn and talking to Sheriff Oliver about the animal's disposition.

"You should go, Marvin," she murmured. "Take these people up to my place. You'll find a cache of guns and ammunition under the floorboards."

He spun around fast and almost spat out the words. "Forget it! If you're going back to Ballantyne, I'm going with you."

"You can't! Someone has to take these people to safety."

"You think for one second I'd let you go back alone? Thanks a lot. You need a continuous line of hearts. That means you can't do it alone—assuming this crackpot scheme of yours actually works."

Just then, Matilda strode over to them. "What's going on? What's the holdup?"

"Ida and I are going back to Ballantyne," Marvin informed her. "We're going to try to find a way to break the bubble."

Out of nowhere, Reverend Sherman materialized behind Marvin like a shade risen from the grave. "I'm going with you."

"I'm going, too," Matilda added. "I never did run from a fight yet and I'm not about to start."

Marvin strode over to Sheriff Oliver. "Forget the horse, Sheriff. We're going back to Ballantyne to find a way to destroy that bubble and you're coming with us."

The sheriff stiffened, but just as fast, his shoulders relaxed. "All right. Count me in."

Marvin turned to Slim. "You take Sadie up to Granite Ridge. Wait there. We'll meet you there when we finish."

"I ain't waiting anywhere. You aren't doing this without me." Sadie glanced over at Ida. "You'll need me to pull you out if you get sucked into that thing again."

Ida's heart overflowed with relief and gratitude when Sheriff Oliver, Sadie, and Marvin strode back to where she stood. They closed in a circle. Their faces set in inflexible resolve for what they were about to do.

Slim watched them in mounting desperation. When the other six reassembled around Ida, he slumped. He raised his arms and let his hands slap against his thighs. "Aw, what the hell! Put the horse away, Max. It looks like we don't need it after all."

Max frowned at them. "Doesn't any of you need a horse at all?"

"Nope," Marvin replied. "Thanks anyway."

Max smacked his lips in exasperation and led the animal back into the barn. Slim joined the others and they faced each other more certain than ever.

"I don't think we'll need weapons, either, to tell you the truth," Matilda remarked.

"What if one of the monsters attacks us?" Sadie asked. "What do we do?"

"If Reverend Sherman is right, then tackling it and hugging it should do the trick," Ida replied.

Marvin guffawed. "It isn't much of a plan, is it?"

"We might skip that with the animals," Sheriff Oliver added, "but when it comes to people, we might be able to bring them back by.... I don't know.... just holding them or something."

"Reverend Sherman reacted on instinct to save Marvin and me. Maybe we could try the same thing. He said our hearts have to be pure, so maybe our desire to save the person is what we really need." Ida turned to the preacher. "Does that sound about right to you, Reverend?"

"I'm sure I have no idea, my dear," Reverend Sherman replied. "As I keep telling you, I have never battled this thing before. As you say, I didn't think when I grabbed you. I wanted to save you. I didn't think of anything else."

"What about Ballantyne?" Sheriff Oliver asked. "How do we burst the bubble to free the town?"

No one knew how to answer. "Maybe we'll know once we get there," Ida suggested.

"So that's it?" Slim demanded. "We're going back there with this pathetic excuse for a plan?"

"Looks like it," Marvin replied.

Ida scanned the group one more time, but she didn't see anybody backing out. Sadie was actually smiling and Matilda and Sheriff Oliver looked happy, too. Ida herself felt lighter, now that she held out some hope for getting rid of the bubble. Even if she failed, at least she could say she tried.

Just then, Beatrice bustled up to them. She shoved a wrapped package into Matilda's hands. "At least have something to eat and sit a spell before you go off again. I don't like sending you out there on an empty stomach."

"Thanks, but I don't think I could eat anything right now." Matilda tried to hand the package back. "I appreciate your effort, but....."

"I'll take it." Sadie snatched the package from her. She sat down on the chopping block while she ripped the wrapping off. "I'm starving."

"You could eat in a hurricane," Slim complained.

"I'm gonna fill up, too." Marvin squatted down next to Sadie. "Gotta keep our strength up."

The package contained a large, steaming meat pie. A few of the others migrated nearer when they saw Marvin and Sadie eating it. Matilda scowled. "How can you eat at a time like this?"

"How can I *not* eat?" Marvin took a lump of crust from Sadie. "It wouldn't do to collapse from hunger in the middle of our campaign."

In a moment, Sheriff Oliver, Slim, and Reverend Sherman took their places around the chopping block, too. Slim sat on the ground. Sheriff Oliver and Reverend Sherman perched on the edge of the water trough.

Marvin grabbed a bucket and turned it upside down next to him. "Take a seat, Ida. Even if you aren't hungry, at least take a load off while you wait. You're making me nervous standing over there."

Ida sank onto the bucket. She found it difficult to let her guard down even in this relaxed environment. She was in no immediate danger, but she kept looking around for some monster to attack her without warning.

"This is a really good pie," Sadie exclaimed. "I haven't tasted anything like this since I left home in Kentucky."

"You never told me you were from Kentucky," Matilda returned. "Why didn't you say?"

"Probably so she wouldn't have to explain why your meat pie isn't the best she ever ate," Slim teased.

"*You* said my meat pie was the best *you* ever ate," Matilda countered. "Was that a lie?"

"Call it a little piece of diplomacy for the sake of domestic bliss."

The others laughed. Marvin turned to Ida. "What did you mean at the school when you said none of us was without sin? I can't imagine you committing any sin. You're an angel."

She looked away. "I'm far from an angel."

"That's impossible. You're as pure as the driven snow."

She couldn't appreciate the compliment. "You only think that because you don't know me very well."

"What do you mean? What did you ever do wrong? Did you snitch a cookie when you were little?"

Her gaze migrated back toward Ballantyne. "I killed my husband."

A chilly silence fell over the group. Marvin broke it by choking on his pie. "I'm sorry. I shouldn't have asked."

"It's all right. It was ten years ago. I guess that's why I spend so much time at the ranch and don't come to town as much as I might."

"How did you escape prison?" Sheriff Oliver asked. "Or hanging?"

"Sheriff!" Matilda snapped. "Mind your own business."

"It's okay," Ida interrupted. "I don't mind talking about it. I haven't talked to anyone about it since it happened. I guess so much time has passed that I don't mind so much now."

Marvin looked up. "So what happened?"

"He got drunk and attacked me. He tried to kill me. He had his Bowie knife to my throat and was about to do it. I grabbed one of his pistols from his holster and shot him in the chest. That was before you came to town, Sheriff. Old Pete Stanley was the sheriff then and he decided it was self-defense."

"How could he be certain?" Sheriff Oliver asked. "He had only your word for it."

"The house was destroyed and I was covered in bruises and scratches—plus I had a cut across my neck from the knife. I ran away as soon as the gun went off and I ran all the way to town in the middle of a downpour. Matilda found me on the back steps of the saloon and she took me in. She called the sheriff and Sheriff Stanley went out to the house. He found the place a wreck and my husband dead. It was pretty clear what happened."

Another dangerous silence fell over the group. Matilda looked down at her hands. None of the others would look at Ida, but she felt better. She'd been carrying that dirty little secret for ten years. Now it was out in the open and she wasn't ashamed anymore. She did what she had to do and she saved her own life. That was enough for her.

Marvin cleared his throat with difficulty and stood up. "Welp, it looks like we got our work cut out for us in town. Let's do this, people. We got a bubble to pop."

# Chapter 8

M arvin stuck close to Ida on the way back to Ballantyne. After hearing the story of her husband's death, he was more certain than ever he wanted her next to him when it came time to tackle that bubble. Instead of spoiling his opinion of her, he respected her more than ever.

The others walked straighter and faster than when they left town. They didn't dawdle and no one looked right or left. No one appeared overly concerned with protecting their backs anymore. That time was long over.

The bubble shimmered brighter with the sunlight coming from behind the friends. The bubble's curved, iridescent sides reflected prismatic colors that blinded and befuddled Marvin if he looked at it too long. He kept thinking again and again that it looked like swirled onyx. The patterns fascinated him. He had to concentrate hard to unfocus his eyes or pay attention to something else.

He checked the way ahead for any sign of changed animals or people, but the area seemed oddly quiet all of a sudden. He didn't hear screams, bellows, or blows the way he did before. That might be because he was more afraid before and fear made them sounded louder, but he didn't think so. Ballantyne was definitely quieter now. Was every living thing in town finally dead?

When the group arrived at the courthouse, Sheriff Oliver waved everyone into it. He led them upstairs to the second floor and down a carpeted corridor to the judge's chambers.

A balcony off the back wall overlooked town. The bubble blocked their view of Main Street. The friends lined up behind the railing and surveyed the bubble from above.

Monsters, transfigured people, and objects carried on their bloody massacre inside its margins. If anything, more combatants than ever marauded all over Main Street. They hunted anything that moved.

A wolf hunched its spiked back over a fanged goat sprawled beneath it. While the friends watched, a wooden laundry paddle somersaulted from over by the jail. It pegged its pointed edge into the wolf's ghastly form.

The paddle set to work hammering its corner into the wolf's skull. The creature whipped around snarling through its teeth. It let out a vicious snarl and snapped its grinning jaws at the paddle.

The goat saw its chance and struck out with its hooves. It impaled the wolf, and between the goat and the paddle, they brought the attacker down. All over Main Street, bloody murder unfolded in every gruesome scene imaginable.

"It can't be as easy as that," Ida murmured from Marvin's left side. "It can't be as simple as keeping contact with each other."

"We'll be taking our lives in our hands going in there," Sheriff Oliver remarked. "I don't care what Reverend Sherman says. I don't see it working. Those things aren't real. Nothing could be as bad as this. He was drunk when he said those monsters were there all the time."

Marvin glanced at the preacher to see how he would take this, but Reverend Sherman didn't react. He didn't seem to hear. He gazed down at the nightmarish scene along with the others. If he was rethinking his statements about the bubble being some kind of reflection of society's evils, he didn't show it.

In that moment, Marvin agreed with Ida and Sheriff Oliver. The bubble wasn't some kind of religious insight into the ills of humanity. This was something a thousand times worse.

Marvin himself was inclined to agree with Ida's earlier statement about the bubble. It must have come from Hell Itself. Nothing else made sense and he didn't see anything defeating it, least of all some paltry notion of human connection.

Human connection didn't make a dent in evil any other time. Why should now make any difference just because these people wanted it to and because Reverend Sherman said it would? That was the most ridiculous notion Marvin could think of.

"So what's the plan?" Matilda asked. "We aren't walking in there without a plan."

No one answered. In that awful silence, everyone faced up to the fact that they had absolutely nothing to fight this thing with. Fighting couldn't defeat it. Nothing could.

Marvin couldn't let that silence linger. He had to break it, even if it meant turning these friends against him. "I'm no angel, either. I'm a sinner, too."

Ida groaned. "Just don't tell me you killed your wife. I couldn't stand that."

"I didn't kill her. *She* tried to kill *me*. She lost her mind after she gave birth. She blamed me for ruining her life. She imagined people coming after her and stalking her in the night. She thought they were out to kill her. Eventually, she started to believe *I* was trying to kill her, too. She stole my gun while I slept, and after I woke up, she turned it on me. I stopped her and took the gun away from her, but later, while I was eating, she yanked the gun from my holster. She ran across the room and shot the baby in his cradle. I tried to stop her then, too, but she turned the gun on herself and shot herself."

Those words fell from the balcony. The bubble swallowed them along with the rest of the evil. In a way, the bubble left the world cleansed of that particular abomination.

He glanced down the row one more time to find Ida looking up at him. Her eyes swam with tears, but her countenance shone with such a heavenly light that his heart lightened. She slipped her hand into his and he felt the hardened calluses on her palm. "Thank you for telling me."

"I'm glad you know. I couldn't go in there without you knowing."

She squeezed his hand and smiled. That smile, with the afternoon sun glinting in her unshed tears, meant more to him than all the comfort in the world.

"If we need a plan," Sheriff Oliver began, "I say we go in there keeping contact with each other all the time. We get hold of the first person we can find and hold onto them, too. We see if this pure heart stuff actually works."

"And if it does?" Slim asked. "Then what?"

"We remove the person from the bubble and send them either to the Lytle farm or to Ida's place on Granite Ridge."

"That's it?" Sadie asked. "We remove people from the bubble one after the other? That's our whole plan?"

"Do you have another one?" Sheriff Oliver asked.

"What if it doesn't work?" Matilda asked.

"Then we leave. If it doesn't work the first time, we leave the bubble—all of us. We take ourselves up to Granite Ridge and we do whatever we have to do to protect ourselves. That's it. If we can't save anyone else, then we have no choice but to save ourselves."

"You're forgetting one thing." Marvin heard the words coming out of his mouth. They sounded far away after what he said a moment ago. "What if keeping contact with each other doesn't work, either? What if we turn into monsters, too?"

"Then we haven't lost anything. We won't know the difference."

"We'll have lost our lives," Matilda pointed out.

"We might do that anyway. At least we tried."

Ida nodded. "That's as good a plan as any. I'm ready to go along with it."

Slim squinted at the bubble. "I don't see any people in there. I see a lot of animals and tools and stuff, but no people."

"Maybe they're hunting outside the bubble," Sadie suggested.

"Either way, we have to keep contact with each other at all times." Ida looked up at Reverend Sherman, but when he still didn't offer any suggestions or get involved in the conversation, she left him alone. "What about finding our way out again? When I was in the bubble before, I couldn't see it. There was no sign that the bubble was ever there."

"Are you sure?" Sadie asked. "It must have been there."

"We could rope ourselves to something outside the bubble," Sheriff Oliver replied. "We could tie one end of a rope to the hitching post in front of the dry goods store and the other end to ourselves. We could use the same rope to tie ourselves together so there's no chance we could get separated."

"You mean like mountain climbers?" Matilda teased.

"I don't hear anybody else coming up with a plan."

"It won't work," Ida countered. "The rope will either break or vanish. We won't be able to find our way out. We won't be able to find the bubble at all."

"Well, how the hell are we supposed to destroy the thing if we can't see it?" Sheriff Oliver demanded.

"I'm just saying," Ida replied. "I was inside that thing. I know what I saw."

"Maybe none of us knows what they're seeing," Matilda pointed out. "We're taking the word of a drunken lout as guidance from Heaven. Maybe all this tripe about keeping contact with each other is just the ravings of a sauced lunatic."

"That's what I'm talking about. Something as watery as that couldn't possibly be strong enough to defeat this thing." Marvin twisted his neck toward Reverend Sherman. "No offense, Reverend."

Reverend Sherman still didn't answer. He stared at the bubble without blinking. Did it hypnotize him, too? Did he even know enough to look away? Maybe that was why the world's evils filled his mind so much of the time. He didn't know how to look away or to think about anything else. They must have driven him completely out of his mind.

"Well, if we're going to try this, we better get the show on the road," Matilda clipped. "I don't want to be anywhere near this town when the sun goes down."

At her word, the group turned away. Without a word, they wound their way to the ground floor and outside. They assembled on Main Street in plain view of the bubble and its resident horrors.

Sheriff Oliver went into the back of the courthouse and came back with a length of rope. He held it up. "It might not work, but we can give it a shot."

He threaded one end of the rope through his belt loops. Then he approached Marvin and started winding the rope's length through Marvin's belt loops, too. Marvin turned his face away with a pained expression. "Just rope me together with Ida, will you?"

Sadie and Matilda laughed at him. "He's facing certain death and he wants you to rope him to a woman. So typical."

"I don't blame him," Slim interjected. "If I had my choice, I'd be roped together with Ida, too."

Matilda punched his arm, but Sheriff Oliver kept working steadily. He tied the four men together first. He clearly wanted to do the chivalrous thing and tie the three women in the center of that circle, but when he got Sadie and Matilda into position, Matilda's copious bulk stopped him from wedging Ida in there, too.

In the end, Sheriff Oliver tied Ida at the edge between Marvin and Slim. This arrangement brought gales of laughter from everyone involved...except Reverend Sherman, who was still somewhere else.

Ida blushed and lifted her eyelashes to peek at Marvin. "Sorry about this."

"Don't even think about trying anything, man," Marvin snapped over her shoulder at Slim. "I've still got some buckshot in this gun of mine and I'm not afraid to use it."

"I'm sure you aren't," Slim muttered.

"Don't worry about Slim," Matilda chimed in. "I'll make sure he minds his manners."

The others laughed again. That laughter sounded strange standing so close to the bubble, but in a way, it was the only sane reaction to the situation. Feral shrieks and guttural snarls mingled with thumps, blasts, and crunches coming from right inside the bubble. The only reactions left were laughter or tears.

Sheriff Oliver finally tied himself into the last place and lashed the rope's other end to a nearby hitching post. He wrapped the group so tight that no one could move. The outer ring consisting of Ida, Marvin, Slim, Sheriff Oliver, and Reverend Sherman all pointed their weapons outward.... except Reverend Sherman. Sheriff Oliver had left their arms free so they could shoot in any direction at will.

"All right," Sheriff Oliver murmured. "Let's go."

He shouldered his rifle and trained it on the bubble. Marvin shifted his shotgun into position, but when he moved around Ida, he discovered her looking up at him. Her eyes spoke volumes and he understood her perfectly. They both knew beyond doubt that this wasn't going to work.

Something prickly brushed Marvin's cheek as he crossed the bubble's outer rim and the rope's pressure vanished from his waist. The next minute, he was standing inside the bubble. Ida was right. The rope was gone.

The group disintegrated for a moment as everyone looked around. They took in the sheer devastation of the strange landscape. They were in a completely unknown city. Ida was right about that, too. They should have listened to her.

The moment the group lost contact with each other, a sick feeling came into Marvin's stomach. What was it? It felt like he'd eaten something rotten and now it was.....

"Quick!" Matilda grabbed him and yanked him forward. "Get in contact with each other. Reform the circle!"

The friends shot together. Without the rope to hold them, they grappled their arms around each other and held on. Marvin gripped a fistful of Ida's dress on one side and the sheriff's vest on the other. Slim grabbed him with one hand and wrapped his other arm around Reverend Sherman's bony skeleton.

Marvin hugged these people as though his life depended on it even though he still didn't believe this keeping contact with each other thing would do anything. He didn't care anymore if it did. He didn't want to let go of them for anything.

Now everyone gawked at the surroundings at their leisure and it didn't look any more promising with them in contact with each other. Devastating explosions and rapid gunfire punctuated the air from not far away. He'd never heard anything like it. It struck terror into his heart so he wanted to break and run.

There was nowhere to run. The friends must have moved a foot away from the bubble at the most, but none of them could see it no matter which way they turned. They were utterly stranded here with no way out.

# Chapter 9

Ida let out a tortured sigh. The group saw what she saw inside the bubble, but that fact didn't cheer her up in the slightest. None of them would be coming to the rescue now. No one outside knew where they were. There was no one on the outside to pull them out.

She tugged at Marvin and tried to drag the group toward the sidewalk. "Let's get off the street."

Sadie cast a petrified look over her shoulder. "Are we still gonna try to find any people?"

"What kind of people live in this place?" Slim curled his lip at the hunks of twisted metal blockading the street. "This place looks like a battlefield."

"It is one." Ida pricked up her ears and listened to the explosions. "The shots are getting closer. Come on. Let's take shelter in one of the....."

Before she finished speaking, a crowd of men catapulted around the nearest building. They flooded the street with bullets whizzing all around them.

They all wore the same uniform. Random patterns of green and brown blotches covered their pants, jackets, and the helmets on their heads. Some even had green and brown paint smeared on their faces. They all carried rifles and they raced straight for the astonished friends.

Gunfire chased them into the street, but Ida couldn't see where it was coming from. The strange men didn't even bother to look behind them. They scattered in all directions and vanished into the buildings on both sides.

Ida opened her mouth to call instructions to her friends when a high-pitched whistle cut the air. It whined closer and then, out of nowhere, a massive blast shattered the pavement a few yards away.

Destroyed rubble peppered Ida's face, arms, and back as she whirled away from the explosion. She barely turned her head aside to avoid a boulder-sized rock twirling past her ear. "Run!" she thundered. "In here!"

She pulled at the group one more time but, to her horror, the party fragmented into seven separate people. Everyone forgot to hold onto each other. They broke and fled, each going in a different direction.

Ida hesitated a fraction of a second scrambling to grab them and pull them with her, but five more blasts erupted out of the torn pavement down the street. In an instant, the smooth surface ruptured into a mound of craggy wreckage.

Marvin barreled through the flying rock and debris and seized Ida around the torso. "Move it!" He shoved her toward the building where she'd been trying to steer the friends, but she didn't see anyone in sight.

Constant crashes and blasts ripped the air. Gravel and fragments pattered against the walls. Marvin and Ida dove behind the nearest heap. They huddled under their arms for any shelter.

Ida peeked up between concussions. The soldiers hunkered in crannies and hiding places all over the street. Five occupied the building right across the street. The blown-out walls revealed everything inside.

While she and Marvin watched, two men rested their rifles on piles of stone. They sighted down their barrels and fired at something Ida couldn't see. Their guns fired unimaginably fast—much faster than any gun Ida had ever seen. The soldiers shouted to each other in a language she didn't recognize. Where in the name of God was she?

Marvin got her attention by tugging at her arm. He jerked his chin backward, and when she followed his gaze, she noticed a section of wall missing behind them. He motioned for her to come with him while he crawled toward it.

Daylight shone from outside. She hesitated, but when another whistling projectile plummeted from the sky and shattered the street to smithereens, she backed away. Ida and Marvin inched to the opening. Through a gap in the bricks, she peeked into another street—an empty one.

She looked back in time to see another group of soldiers in different uniforms invade the street where the friends just stood. The newcomers drove the first squad before them and fired into the buildings mowing down anyone who didn't escape in time.

Ida dove through the opening after Marvin. They scrambled to a deserted side street with no one around. No soldiers from either army. No monsters. No friends. No one.

Marvin grabbed her hand and drew her to the end of the block. The intersection was vacant, too. Ida kept checking everywhere, but no one moved in any direction. Not seeing anyone only made her more tense and nervous. Where was everyone? Where were Sadie, Slim, Matilda, and Sheriff Oliver? Would she ever see them again?

She and Marvin set off to their left. Ida had no idea where they were going. Where didn't seem to matter anymore. They were alone in this strange world.

For all she knew, whatever force separated the friends from Ballantyne also separated her and Marvin from the rest of the group. Some invisible barrier might have transported the other four to a completely different world far away from here. Then again, maybe she and Marvin were the ones who were somewhere else while the other four were still...wherever it was.

She didn't have time to think about that. She and Marvin kept hold of each other's hands, but Ida didn't mind. She wanted nothing in the world but to hold onto him. She didn't want to let go of him—not ever.

They walked five blocks without seeing anyone. The sounds of battle diminished into the background, but that didn't quiet Ida's nerves. Silence meant nothing. The danger didn't abate no matter how far away they got.

Marvin stopped at the next intersection and they both looked around them. "Any ideas?" he asked. "We could try to find a safe place to hunker down until we find a way to get back to Ballantyne."

"*How* will we get back to Ballantyne? We would have to find the bubble and it isn't here." She looked behind her for the thousandth time. "We don't know if another bubble will ever occur, much less if it will appear here."

"Then that's all the more reason we should find a safe place to go to ground. Come on. Let's get out of here."

They started walking again. What else was there to do? After what she'd seen in Ballantyne, Ida wasn't convinced going back there was the right thing anyway. One place seemed as dangerous as the next. If there was such a thing as a safe place anymore, she'd be as likely to find one here as there.

She followed Marvin blindly. Her hand in his lulled her into a stupor. She could let him lead and forget about everything for a little while, at least. He seemed to fall into the same leader-follower pattern. He didn't bring her back to the present by asking questions or talking to her.

He stopped at another random intersection. She no longer knew or cared where she was in comparison to where they first arrived. He opened his mouth to speak when they both heard voices nearby. Marvin cocked his head and listened. "Do you hear that?"

"It's coming from over there, behind those buildings." Ida perked up. "Maybe some other people are stranded in this city."

Marvin listened again. "They're speaking another language."

"Do you recognize it? I don't."

"No. It isn't any language I ever heard before. Let's go see what they're up to."

The pair tiptoed toward the sound. They scooted to the nearest wall. They flattened themselves against it and peered around the corner. Ida's heart stood still when she saw another bunch of soldiers. They belonged to the second group, the ones who attacked and drove the first group away.

They held their rifles in front of them while another squad herded a cluster of civilians into view. These people wore ragged clothes. Grime and mud smeared their faces and hands and necks. Their hair hung in mats and some of them looked emaciated.

The civilians—if that was what they were—walked with their fingers laced on top of their heads and Ida choked down a gasp when she saw women in the group. The soldiers lined these prisoners against the nearest building and stood back to hold them at gunpoint.

Ida nearly screamed when the soldiers opened fire and gunned down the prisoners without ceremony. She clapped her hand over her mouth to stifle a strangled cry. Marvin grabbed her and pushed her out of sight to stop her from doing anything to attract attention.

She clutched at Marvin and buried her eyes in his shirt as one barrage of gunfire after another ripped around the corner. She couldn't look. She couldn't even think about what those soldiers just did. They murdered those poor people in cold blood. Why?

Marvin's arms shook holding onto her. She might have lost consciousness, but in a second, he pushed her off. He made her stand up straight and she shook the fog out of her head.

She threw back her head....and froze. Another group of soldiers surrounded her and Marvin. They aimed their guns at the shocked pair and the soldiers' faces expressed not the slightest trace of compassion or interest in why Marvin and Ida might be there.

Marvin stiffened at her side and his fingers crept into her grasp. She squeezed them and their fingers threaded together. The soldiers charged the pair and tore all their weapons away. They even took Marvin's pistols and his Bowie knife. The soldier in front sliced his rifle barrel to one side and barked something in his strange language.

Ida's strength failed her. She stumbled after Marvin walking around the corner into the scene of murder and bloodshed she just witnessed.

The soldiers surrounded the pair only a few feet from the pile of bodies near the wall. One soldier who acted like their leader kept snapping orders that neither Ida nor Marvin understood. Eventually, he waved his hand upward and they raised their arms. They laced their fingers behind their heads the way the prisoners did. Ida didn't like where this was going at all.

The soldiers didn't shoot, though. They surrounded Marvin and Ida and held them at gunpoint, but at least they didn't back them against the wall. The squad carried on a rapid discussion amongst themselves trying to agree on something and make a decision.

All at once, a shout went up from a different direction. More soldiers appeared guiding another group of prisoners. They prodded everyone into one cluster and Ida almost got herself shot when she screamed again and tried to charge the newcomers. "Matilda! Sheriff!"

The soldiers pushed Matilda, Sheriff Oliver, Reverend Sherman, and Slim into the circle. Only Sadie was missing. The friends grabbed each other and held on for dear life. "Are you okay?" Sadie squeaked.

"We thought we'd never see you again!" Slim exclaimed. "Thank God you're alive!"

"We thought the same thing about you," Ida replied. "I feared the worst."

"Where's Sadie?" Marvin asked.

"We have no idea," Matilda replied. "We haven't seen her since we first split up."

"We better stick together from now on." Sheriff Oliver cast a harsh glance toward their captors. "I wish I knew what they plan to do with us."

"Can you understand their language?" Marvin asked Reverend Sherman. "Do you recognize it?"

Reverend Sherman shook his head. "I've never heard it before. It sounds vaguely Middle Eastern or perhaps a derivation of Russian, but I can't be certain."

"It doesn't matter what language it is if none of us can communicate with them," Matilda pointed out. "What are they doing here, anyway?"

"They shot those people." Ida pointed to the corpses littering the street. "They lined them all up and shot them, but they aren't doing that with us."

"Who are these people they brought in with you?" Marvin examined the strangers in the circle. They wore the same ragged clothes. They looked and smelled as dirty and poverty-stricken as the soldiers' unfortunate victims.

"We never saw them before," Sheriff Oliver replied. "Reverend Sherman and I ended up hiding in the same spot. When they captured us, Matilda and Slim were already there and so were these people."

"The same thing happened to us," Matilda added. "The soldiers put us in a group with these people after they captured us. The soldiers must have captured them first."

The soldier's argument rose to a fevered pitch. They shouted and gesticulated wildly. Two men charged each other and started throwing their fists. Their rifles dangled by their straps while the combatants punched, kicked, and did their best to grapple each other off their feet.

Ida gaped at them in stark horror as they started to change. Their faces elongated and their mouths stretched. They bared their teeth trying to overcome each other and their teeth lengthened into fangs. Their eyes darkened, swelled, and changed into smooth, shiny orbs gleaming with murderous hate.

All over the street, the other soldiers attacked each other. Their grimaces transformed them into monsters. Their fingers gnarled into claws and their limbs bent at grotesque angles.

All at once, one of the others drew a pistol from his belt and pointed it at another. Before he could fire, the leader intervened. He rushed the gunman and slapped the weapon to the ground.

The gun slammed onto the pavement and went off. The prisoners jumped and the friends crowded together even tighter. Marvin put his arm around Ida and the others took hold of each other. They hung on the way they did when they were roped together.

The soldiers froze and the transformation turning them into monsters vanished as quickly as it began. The gunshot startled them into cutting off their squabble. They became regular men again. The leader roared at them all in a rage. For a moment, his furious visage started to distort. His monstrous expression threatened to break out over his whole body and turn him into a fiend, but none of his men engaged with him like this. They turned away, shamefaced, and his anger died.

"They don't seem to be getting along very well," Slim murmured. "We might be able to use that to our advantage."

"Don't even think about it," Matilda whispered. "If they caught us trying to escape, they would shoot us for sure."

"They may be planning to shoot us anyway," Sheriff Oliver pointed out. "If they are, then trying to escaping would be the smartest course."

Ida glanced around at her friends. None of them even mentioned the soldiers turning into monsters. She looked over at Marvin. "Did you see that?"

He didn't hear her. A new sound drew everyone's attention to where a tall, smooth, immaculately groomed chestnut stallion strutted into view. The man on the horse's back wore a heavily decorated uniform. Silver braid draped from his epaulets. A triangular hat perched on his neatly clipped hair.

The strange prisoners groaned and turned their faces away. One of the women prisoners choked back sobs. The soldiers straightened up immediately and every one of them turned to face the officer.

# Chapter 10

The officer reined his horse to a halt. The prisoners huddled beneath him and he gazed down at his helpless captives. Only Marvin returned that gaze. Ida cowered against him and Marvin held her close to protect her from this idiot.

The officer searched the prisoners, but when he noticed Marvin glaring at him, the man turned all his attention on Marvin. He said something in his own language, but his tone told Marvin he expected an answer.

"I don't understand you," Marvin told him. "We don't come from this country."

The officer's eyebrows shot up. "English? You speak English."

"Yes, we do. We don't understand your language." Marvin frowned. "How do you know English?"

"That is my own affair." The officer swung out of his saddle. One of the soldiers took the animal's bridle while the officer strolled back and forth in front of the prisoners. "You are not members of the underground movement."

"What underground movement? We don't know anything about your war. We aren't from here. I told you that."

The officer stopped in front of him and let his eyes slide down Marvin's clothes and then down Ida's. "You certainly dress strangely. Where do you come from, then—England?"

"England!" Marvin snorted. "We're Americans. Can't you see that?"

The officer sneered. "Americans." The listening soldiers burst into insolent laughter.

The officer rounded on Marvin with his thin lips curved into a toothy grin. "So the filthy Americans decided to interfere in our war after all by sending spies to infiltrate our enemies. I should have known. The generals will be most interested to hear about this."

"We aren't spies," Marvin snapped. "Do you seriously think we would be dressed like this if we were spies? We would dress to blend in with the locals. Jesus, use your brain."

"Easy," Matilda murmured in his ear.

Marvin wrestled his temper under control. He couldn't afford to insult this man. The officer didn't seem to mind, though. He strode back and forth once or twice and then stopped again. "It doesn't matter what you're doing here. You will never report your findings to your superiors."

He motioned to the squad leader who first captured Marvin and Ida. The man moved in and aimed his gun at Marvin while the officer walked away and remounted his horse. The animal stamped and snorted while the rider settled in his saddle.

The officer cast another indulgent glance over the scene and took his reins. He got ready to steer the animal away when an ear-splitting shriek rent the air. Everyone whirled around as five more soldiers staggered into sight wrestling a disheveled figure between them.

The first thing Marvin saw was a torn dress half-concealing a scrawny female figure. Bright red hair whipped across the prisoner's cheeks and hid her face. She struggled, kicked, and fought so hard it took all five soldiers working together just to hold onto her.

They wrestled her around the corner. She gave a vicious yank to her left and their grip ripped her dress even more. It draped off her shoulder and threatened to expose her whole chest.

She screeched louder than ever and jerked the other way. Her hair slapped over her shoulder and the friends stared at her in shock. Sadie. She didn't see anything but the soldiers holding her. Her insane eyes skimmed the area, but she didn't recognize anyone she knew.

In that moment, her twisted countenance changed before Marvin's eyes. Her gnashing teeth sharpened into fangs and her screams escalated to a blood-curdling howl. She contorted back the other way and lunged for her nearest captor. She made a dive for his neck and snapped her jaws to rip his throat out.

The target dodged just in time and attacked her just as hard. His countenance screwed into a mask of fiendish rage and his whole body changed in the blink of an eye. He roared with a voice of thunder and wielded his rifle on high to bludgeon Sadie to death.

She exploded into a full monster like those on the streets of Ballantyne. Every trace of the pretty bar girl from the saloon vanished without a trace. Her skin darkened into mottled scales and her joints swelled to knobs. Her eyes went black and sightless.

The other four soldiers restraining her transformed at the same time. They piled on top of her snapping, spitting, shrieking, and clawing. They clubbed at her with their rifles and one of them seized a handful of her hair with long claws.

The other soldiers already in the street changed, too. Their monstrous visages leered at the scene. Bloodlust glinted in their eyes. They advanced to join their comrades. Even the officer on horseback transformed into a monster with a broad, fanged mouth.

The instant the attacker grabbed Sadie's hair, she retaliated with a vengeance. She rounded on him and, with superhuman strength, she yanked her other arm out of her captor's grip. She chopped the arm holding her hair and the bone cracked so loud Marvin heard it across the street.

The monster's hand released and he let out a spine-chilling screech. With another impossible struggle, Sadie wrenched out of their hold and darted forward. She plunged into the street, but she didn't run like a human woman. She bounded on all fours like something half-animal and half-fiend.

She barreled straight for the officer and took a flying leap for him. She levitated off the ground and would have tackled him out of his saddle, but he saw her coming. He rotated sideways as she streaked for his head and he pulled what looked like a silver-handled walking cane from a hidden place on his saddle.

Sadie soared into reach and he clubbed her down with a cruel sideswipe across the neck. She flopped sideways and crashed to the pavement in front of his horse.

She bounced up gnashing all her glistening fangs. She reared back for another assault, but the animal also transformed into a monster. Its face elongated into a macabre version of a horse. Fangs stuck out of a mouth too big for them and spikes ran down its head and neck in place of a mane.

The creature reared on his hind legs. The officer balanced on the demon's back and the horse struck its pointed hooves down hard on Sadie's head and shoulders. The creature pummeled her to the ground and stamped on her several times.

The monstrous officer grinned and cackled with deadly glee. He made no attempt to stop his horse from killing her.

Marvin glanced around for any way to help Sadie. He caught a split-second's view of the buildings and ruins surrounding their location. It happened so fast he wasn't sure afterward whether he really saw what he thought he saw. The destroyed buildings changed and he stared at the blasted storefronts and buildings along Main Street in Ballantyne.

He didn't have time even to blink before the apparition vanished and he was back where he started. That fast, the monsters changed back into men. The officer sat in his saddle as composed and groomed as before. The horse backed away from Sadie's fallen form.

The officer sliced his finger at the soldiers, who were all back to normal, too. He spoke to them in their own language and then reined his horse away. The animal pranced around the corner and disappeared taking the officer with it.

The soldiers prodded the friends with their rifles. Marvin stumbled forward still holding onto Ida, but when he tried to walk where they directed him, the squad leader grabbed him. He pointed at Sadie and said something to Marvin.

Marvin checked the man's expression and the man repeated what he said. He pointed to Sadie again and gesticulated toward where his men were steering the rest of the prisoners.

Marvin didn't want to believe it, but when he still hesitated, the squad leader took his arm and physically dragged him over to Sadie. He pointed to her for the third time.

Marvin bent down. Blood trickled from her head and a nasty gash on one of her shoulders, but she was alive and breathing, even if she was unconscious. She was as beautiful, youthful, and milky-white as she was in Ballantyne. She wasn't a monster anymore.

He kept his eyes on the squad leader while he wedged his arms under her. The squad leader nodded and pointed toward the rest of the group. Marvin hoisted Sadie into his arms and carried her back to where the soldiers were marching the captives away. The squad leader relaxed considerably once Marvin got Sadie into the group. This must be what he wanted.

Under heavy guard, the soldiers escorted the friends through miles of city. After a while, the buildings got shorter and closer to the ground. No matter how far they went the more obvious it became that they were nowhere near Ballantyne. They weren't in the West. They weren't in America at all.

Instead of dusty scrubland outside of town, the paved road wound through lush, green farmland dotted with spreading oak trees. Streams wound through the hills and valleys. A few abandoned farm animals milled around the pastures, but Marvin didn't see any other people.

His arms trembled from the strain of carrying Sadie. After they left the city, he bit the bullet and slung her senseless body over his shoulder. Ida tried to check on Sadie, but no one could do anything on the march.

Miles out of town, the soldiers turned off on a side road that led to a giant camp fenced in barbed wire. Thousands of ragged civilians packed the interior. They all looked as dirty, emaciated, and desperate as the people the soldiers shot in town.

Ramshackle warehouses built in rows dotted the camp. Prisoners meandered in and out and several came to the fence to inspect the new arrivals.

More uniformed soldiers guarded the fence and occupied watchtowers around the perimeter. They opened a gate to let the newcomers in. The escort shoved everyone inside and then left them to their own devices.

Ida guided Marvin to the nearest house and helped him lower Sadie to the ground. As soon as Sadie's weight left his shoulder, Marvin collapsed and slumped against the wooden structure. He groaned and shut his eyes. "How about a nice frosty pitcher of beer for my trouble?"

Ida smiled, but she didn't laugh. "She has a cut along her hairline, but I don't think her skull is broken."

Matilda bent over Sadie, too. "Will she be all right?"

"There's no way of saying." Ida cast an appraising glance around the camp. "It doesn't look like we're going to be able to get a doctor to see her, either."

"Throw in a grilled steak, baked potato, and a big slice of peach pie while you're at it," Marvin told her.

This time, she really did laugh. She swiveled over to him and pushed back his hat to run her slender hand across his forehead. It would have been a motherly touch if her hand hadn't been so callused. "I'll go see about getting you something to eat and drink. You deserve a medal for carrying her all that way."

She walked away. In a second, the crowd of prisoners swallowed her. Marvin watched her go with mixed emotions. She was going in search of food and drink for him after the friends agreed to stick together. He shouldn't have let her go.

Sheriff Oliver, Reverend Sherman, and Slim eased close to Marvin, Sadie, and Matilda. When Marvin scrutinized their faces, he saw traces of doubt and fear that wasn't there before. Did they see the monsters or was Marvin losing his mind?

The sheriff, the preacher, and Slim sat down against the building, too. They lined up and everyone looked out at the camp. A babble of voices nearby made Marvin look that way.

The prisoners spoke a different language—a different language than the soldiers. Another smattering of conversation broke out to Marvin's other side. A bunch of prisoners crowded together all talking fast. They spoke in another language again. Everywhere Marvin turned, he heard different languages and he couldn't understand any of them.

"Where in the name of God are we?" Slim breathed.

"This must be Hell," Reverend Sherman remarked.

As if in answer to his words, the voices to Marvin's right rose in argument. The prisoners bumped their chests together and a few shoved each other. Their faces started to change into monsters, but at that second, another man forced his way into the group. He pushed the adversaries apart and barked at them.

The combatants separated and the conflict died. They were only men. They weren't monsters.

Just then, Ida returned carrying a small metal pot in one hand and a clay jar in the other. She set both down in front of Marvin. "It isn't a steak and baked potato. In fact, I don't think you'll like it at all. It smells foul, but it was all I could find. No one around here speaks English. I finally found someone who understood what I was talking about and he said this is all there is. He said you eat this or you starve. Even the water smells foul, but all the other prisoners are eating and drinking it, so it must be okay."

Marvin raised the pot to his nose and jerked his head away. "Uck! What is that? It's rotten."

"I think it's supposed to be soup." Ida set it aside. She sat down next to him and leaned her back against the wall. "If we're here for any length of time, we might learn to appreciate it as much as they do."

The instant she took her place, a boy weaseled his way out of the throng. He ran up to the friends, pointed at the pot, and started jabbering in some weird tongue. He made gestures and he pulled wild faces.

Ida waved at him and the pot. "Take it. You can have it."

The boy snatched the container and tipped it up. He guzzled the contents right there and then went through an elaborate ritual of licking every droplet out of the bottom. He lowered the empty pot to the ground with a beatific smile on his face. He bowed and said something appreciative to Ida before he made his exit.

"Sweet Jesus!" Reverend Sherman murmured.

"I think you're right, Reverend," Sheriff Oliver remarked. "This must be Hell. We've finally found it. It wasn't in Ballantyne after all. This is the real thing."

A weighty silence fell over the friends. Marvin's blood ran cold, but a wave of warmth ran through him when Ida almost whispered in his ear. "I think I'm losing my mind."

Marvin snapped around to stare at her. It wasn't just him. "You aren't. The same thing happened to me."

"Me, too!" Matilda cried. "I thought I was the only one."

Sheriff Oliver scanned down the line of faces. "Did we all see it?"

"Did you see Ballantyne?" Marvin asked. "Did you see the buildings change into Main Street?"

"I saw it, but I can't think what it means," Matilda replied. "How can *this* be Ballantyne? It makes no sense."

"It seems to change when people start fighting," Sheriff Oliver pointed out. "They turn into monsters and the surroundings change into Ballantyne."

"How is that possible?" Ida asked. "You just said this was Hell, but Ballantyne sure looked like Hell to me. It doesn't make sense that both places would be.....Oh, God! What am I saying? None of this makes sense."

"You're right," Marvin replied. "From everything that's happened, I think we can all forget about what is possible and what is what. None of this fits any concept of reality we can understand."

"How do you explain it, Reverend?" Slim asked. "You said it's always like this. What did you mean? If *you* can't make sense of this, what chance do the rest of us have?"

"What did you mean when you said it's always like this?" Matilda asked.

Reverend Sherman shrugged. "People are monsters. They always have been."

"That doesn't explain anything," Sheriff Oliver snarled. "If you can't help us understand what's happening, then what use are you?"

"It isn't just people turning into monsters," Ida added. "It's birds and objects and children. You can't tell me that sticks of wood are really monsters. You can't tell me dogs and little girls are really monsters waiting to kill people."

"While we're forgetting about making sense of it all," Marvin chimed in, "we might as well forget about Reverend Sherman giving us any explanation. His area of expertise is the Bible and Christianity. He doesn't understand this any better than we do."

Reverend Sherman didn't respond to this. If Marvin's comments offended the preacher, he didn't show it.

Just then, Sadie stirred at Marvin's side. He pivoted around and Ida and Matilda sprang into action. They surrounded Sadie and helped the girl sit up.

Sadie groaned. "What happened? Where are we?"

"That's what we'd all like to know." Matilda stopped her from touching her head. "Don't touch it, honey. You'll get blood all over yourself. Do you have your handkerchief, Reverend? Wet it in some of that water so I can clean this up."

Sadie's eyes cleared while Matilda bathed her forehead in cold water. She looked around her for the first time. Her expression changed and then she flung her arms over her chest. She tried to hide herself from the world even though no one noticed her torn clothes.

"Don't worry, Sadie. You can wear this dress." Ida straightened up and started unlacing her bodice.

"What are you doing?" Sheriff Oliver asked.

"I'm taking my dress off. She's half-naked. We can't leave her like this. Look. The sun is going down. It will be dark soon and we have no idea how these prisoners will behave around a woman."

Sheriff Oliver shot out a hand. "Stop! You can't......!"

He didn't get to Ida quick enough before she pulled her dress over her head to reveal her pants, boots, and chaps underneath. She wore a woolen chemise and full-length petticoat underneath with the skirts tucked into her dead husband's leather belt.

Marvin watched in delight when Sheriff Oliver screamed and covered his eyes to avoid seeing Ida undress. He gaped at her in astonishment when he realized she wasn't naked underneath her dress.

Ida completely ignored him. She gathered the dress into a bunch and slipped it over Sadie's head. Ida tugged it into place and started tightening the bodice laces. "There. That's better, isn't it?"

Sadie sniffed and quavered. She looked awful with blood caking her hair. "Thank you, Ida."

Ida untucked her petticoat and draped it over her pants, but she still didn't look right. Marvin didn't care what she wore. She sat down in front of him and pretended to look at Sadie's cut scalp again. She kept her back to the camp and whispered in an undertone. "If we're going to escape, we should do it soon before we get too weak from hunger or disease. The longer we stay here, the more we'll become like these people. We may even doubt that we ever came from Ballantyne."

"How can we escape?" Sheriff Oliver asked. "We have no weapons and no way of returning to the city."

"We aren't completely helpless." Ida put her hand under her petticoat and into her chemise. She drew out another revolver she kept hidden there. She flashed it to the group and then stowed it in its hiding place.

"Where did you get that?" Matilda exclaimed. "Did you have that ever since we left Ballantyne?"

Ida nodded. "I always carry it—ever since the night my husband died. I never wanted to be without a weapon again."

"That doesn't help us get out of here," Slim countered. "I counted more than thirty guards around the fence and in the watchtowers and we have no idea how many more they'll have patrolling *inside* the fence."

"There aren't any patrolling inside the fence," Ida replied. "I looked when I went to get the food and water. There's no trace of the soldiers. From what I can tell, they keep away from the prisoners. They keep separate unless they're bringing people in or changing shifts."

"That still doesn't help us get *out* of the fence," Sheriff Oliver insisted.

"He's right, Ida," Marvin chimed in. "Even if we could get through the fence, the guards would catch us before we ever got back to the city."

"We don't have to get back to the city," Matilda pointed out. "If we're right, the monsters and Ballantyne will be right here. The next time a fight breaks out and people start trying to kill each other, we'll be back on Main Street."

"What are you talking about?" Sadie asked. "What's all this about monsters and Ballantyne and Main Street?"

Matilda spun around. "You don't know? You didn't see?"

"See what?" Sadie's gaze skipped from one to another. "What are you all talking about?"

The others exchanged glances. Marvin didn't want to be the one to tell her the monsters were back or that murderous intentions would transport them all back to the deadly streets of Ballantyne. He definitely didn't want to be the one to tell her that *she* turned into a monster.

In the end, it was Ida who spoke. "What's the last thing you remember before you passed out? What were you doing?"

Sadie blinked her. She looked down at the ground and blinked again. "I.... I was....."

"We roped ourselves together outside the courthouse," Sheriff Oliver recalled. "You remember that, don't you? Then we stepped inside the bubble and the rope wasn't there anymore."

Sadie nodded. "We were standing there when those soldiers ran over."

"And then that bomb went off and we all scattered," Slim went on. "We all ran off in different directions."

"What do you remember after that?" Ida asked.

"I ran into one of those buildings. I was hiding under a fallen beam. I waited until some other soldiers ran around the corner and chased the first group away. They all left and it got real quiet. I came out and started looking for all of you, but the soldiers came back and caught me."

"Then what?" Marvin asked.

"They were holding onto you and your dress tore," Ida prompted.

Sadie nodded. "They laughed and one of them tried to grab me. I got scared and I started fighting. They started pulling me somewhere and I didn't want to go. I yelled and cursed them, but they didn't listen. Then, they turned a corner and....." She broke off.

Marvin watched the horrified realization dawn in her blue eyes. She jerked back and her eyes shot to Ida's face. "No! It can't be! It couldn't be! Not here."

"I'm afraid so," Reverend Sherman replied. "Even here—especially here."

"After you passed out," Ida went on, "the buildings changed, too. First, the people turned into monsters. Maybe, like the Reverend says, people are more prone to changing. Then the horse changed and then we all saw the buildings change. The city turned back into Ballantyne."

"It only happened for a split second," Marvin reminded her. "The minute everyone started to calm down, it turned back into the city."

"If that's true," Sheriff Oliver remarked, "then we would have to get back into a seriously life-threatening conflict before it would change all the way back into Ballantyne."

Sadie groaned. "God, no! Anything but that."

"Not only that," Ida went on, "it would change back into Ballantyne inside the bubble. It wouldn't be the Ballantyne we all know. We would be surrounded by monsters trying to kill us."

"*We* would turn into monsters, too," Marvin pointed out. "If we were in a situation that dangerous, we might *have* to change into monsters just to survive it. We would have to defend ourselves. We all saw what happened to Sadie. She was fighting monsters and she turned into one to defend herself."

"Oh, please, don't talk like that!" Sadie cried. "I can't stand it."

Ida squeezed her wrist. "No one blames you, sweetie. You did what you had to do. If anything, you helped us by showing us what we can expect if it happens again."

"So what are we going to do about getting out of here?" Sheriff Oliver asked again. "We can't stay here. That's out of the question."

"It's better than turning into monsters," Sadie quavered.

"Or getting killed by monsters," Matilda added.

"We just have to watch our chance," Marvin replied. "We'll all keep our eyes open for any opportunity to break out. That's the best we can do for now."

# Chapter 11

Someone shook Ida awake. She rubbed sleep out of her eyes trying to remember where she was. "Get up, Ida," someone murmured. "We have to go. Come on. Get up."

"Marvin."

"Yeah, it's me. Get up. Come on. You have to hurry."

She followed his guiding hands and clambered to her feet. When she saw where she was, all the horrible events of yesterday came flooding back.

When night fell, the prisoners packed into warehouses lined with bunks three tiers high. Every bunk had at least two people sleeping in them. Many had three already. No one wanted to make room for the newcomers and most couldn't if they had wanted to.

The friends ended up sleeping on the floor in the corner. Ida stretched the stiffness out of her limbs and the others didn't look much better off. Hunger gnawed a hole in her stomach, but she learned quickly enough not to complain or to ask for food. None of the prisoners got any food after the rancid soup she brought back yesterday. Men, women, and children went to bed hungry.

The open door at one end of the building let in the only light and air. The stuffy bunkhouse smelled of countless filthy bodies. Ida was only too glad to head outside. "Where are we going?"

"I don't know," Marvin replied, "but we're moving out. We can't stand around."

As soon as she got outside, she saw he was right. The prisoners assembled by the gate. Uniformed soldiers surrounded them holding everyone at gunpoint while the officer from yesterday rode up and down on his horse like some kind of provincial lord overseeing his serfs.

The prisoners held themselves stiff and silent. No one fidgeted and no one made eye contact with the soldiers. The prisoners trained their unwavering gaze through the gate.

Ida looked around her only long enough to make sure the rest of the friends stayed together. Sadie stumbled. Her skin went greyish pale, but she kept up with the others. Slim put his arm around her shoulder and held her against him to support her.

Marvin and Ida joined hands. Sheriff Oliver shifted his position to the outside and kept scanning the crowd to make sure no one interfered with the group.

"You have your piece?" Marvin whispered in Ida's ear.

She gave him a barely perceptible nod. She didn't have to check to feel the gun tucked inside her chemise. From the looks of things, the prisoners were going outside the fence. If that was true, the possibilities for escape improved considerably.

She took her place in the throng and the friends looked straight ahead along with the rest of the assembly. The soldiers kept pacing and shouting orders Ida didn't understand. She didn't have to understand. All she had to do was follow and copy the other prisoners.

The mob stayed standing there for more than an hour and a half. Ida dared not look around to find out what the holdup was. Soldiers left their posts, went into the camp, and returned only for different soldiers to leave and come back.

The officer kept up his constant back and forth pacing. The horse stamped and rolled his eyes at the crowd. At long last, the order went up and three soldiers opened the gate. They pulled the wire out of the way and the assembled prisoners started forward.

They formed a long column that stretched out as they walked. They crossed the fields and ended up on the same road that brought them here. Ida didn't want to ask the obvious question, but after an hour of walking, Sheriff Oliver eased over to Marvin. "They're taking us back to the city. Why?"

"God only knows," Marvin murmured back.

"There's a railroad track," Ida observed. "Maybe they're taking us to a train station."

"As soon as we get into town, we make a break for it," Marvin suggested. "We can dive into one of the alleys and get away from them. They won't be able to chase us because they'll have to guard the other prisoners."

"They'll shoot at us," Sheriff Oliver pointed out.

"The buildings will give us some cover. Pass the word to the others."

Ida whispered the plan to Slim who told Sadie. "We need some kind of signal to run," Matilda breathed to Marvin when he told her. "We also need a meeting place if we get separated."

"We should break at one of the corners," Slim suggested. "That's a certain number of soldiers who will be out of sight when we run."

"Once we run, we should get as far away from each other as possible," Sheriff Oliver added. "That will give the soldiers too many targets. They won't be able to follow all of us."

"That will make it more difficult to meet up again later," Sadie pointed out. "We might never meet up."

"Here's what we'll do," Ida decided. "We'll scatter and hide. We'll stay out of sight until the column is gone. Then we'll reassemble in the same street where the column was when we split. Does everyone agree?"

The others nodded. "I'll call, 'Now' when it's time to run," Marvin announced. "As soon as I give the word, break and run for it. Just make sure you don't run so far that you can't find your way back to the same street."

The group agreed to this plan. Ida's spirits lifted now that she had something to look forward to. She didn't point out that, if they left the column, they would be moving away from the one source that might actually take them back to Ballantyne. If they were right about how this weird world worked, they needed the conflict of this foreign war to bring them back to the monsters and the bubble.

The walk into town took a thousand times longer than the hike out of it. Ida's nerves stretched to the breaking point waiting for the moment of escape. Time and again, she had to stop herself from taking out her gun and double- and triple-checking that it was loaded and ready to shoot.

The others seemed to brighten up and pay a lot more attention, now that they knew what to expect. Sadie kept her eyes on the road ahead. In a little while, the close neighborhoods and tall buildings of the city came into sight.

If any other prisoners planned to use this opportunity to escape, they kept their intentions hidden. Many fell on the march and gunfire stuttered behind the column. None of the survivors turned around to see what happened to them.

Ida eased closer to Marvin as the buildings got taller. Residential neighborhoods gave way to a dense urban landscape. Explosions and the noise of ongoing battle drifted between the buildings. The high walls prevented Ida from telling which direction it was coming from.

Marvin tightened his grip on her hand until it hurt, but she wouldn't have it any other way. She wanted him holding onto her so he would take her with him when he ran. She didn't want to get separated from him under any circumstances.

The soldiers didn't appear to recognize the danger of anyone escaping. They didn't heighten their vigilance. If anything, they relaxed once they entered the city. They kept less watch on the prisoners and paid more attention to where they were going.

Some of them swung their rifles to their shoulders, but they didn't point them at the prisoners. They aimed outward at abandoned buildings in search of the opposing army personnel.

Ida traced their route. She thought she recognized landmarks from yesterday, but she might have been mistaken. The journey wore on hour after hour and she became more certain than ever that the soldiers were taking the prisoners back almost to the same spot where the friends entered the bubble. Was that possible? Could they be doing that on purpose?

All at once, one of the soldiers yelled. The noise startled Ida out of her thoughts. Marvin stiffened. The whole column came to a halt right there in the middle of the street.

The soldiers rotated to point their guns at the prisoners once again. Shouts and orders rang up and down the column. "What's going on?" Sadie whispered.

"Something's wrong," Marvin muttered. "They wouldn't stop us like this otherwise."

Ida looked behind her, but hundreds of prisoners blocked her from seeing anything. "What do you want to do about breaking out? Should we go now?"

"No. The soldiers are on high alert. They're expecting us to try something now. We would be cut down for sure if we did. Just sit tight. As soon as they straighten out the problem, we'll be on the move again. In a little while, they'll relax again. Then we can...."

A scream broke out of the crowd somewhere behind them. The friends and many prisoners all whirled around, but there was nothing to see. The soldiers left their positions and hurried down the line toward the sound. The officer came cantering into view on his big stallion.

He galloped past going somewhere. For a long moment, silence descended over the scene. Ida faced front waiting for the column to move out again, but in half a second, the soldiers came trooping back.

This time, they walked in a group talking rapidly. The squad leader from yesterday came with them along with the officer still in the saddle. The horse tossed his head and snorted like anything.

They drew level with the friends and then continued on still deep in heated conversation. The officer stopped his horse twenty feet in front of Ida and Marvin. He spat orders to his men and pointed up and down the column. Unfortunately for the friends' plan, the column hadn't turned a single corner. The whole throng of prisoners extended in front of them as far as the eye could see. The soldiers could see everyone plain as day.

Ida groaned inwardly. This delay would only make the soldiers tense. They wouldn't relax their vigilance again. The friends may have missed their chance to escape.

Without warning, four prisoners darted out of the crowd. Before anyone could stop them, they charged the officer's horse. They laid into the animal so fast the soldiers never had a chance to react.

One of the attackers pulled a hidden weapon from somewhere. He slashed the blade along the horse's flank and gutted the creature right then and there. The horse's entrails tumbled to the ground.

The horse reared with a fearful shriek. Blood gushed from the wound and he rolled his eyes in alarm, but his own movement only made the situation worse. He got tangled in his own intestines and tripped himself.

Lightning quick, the other three prisoners rushed in. One of them grabbed the officer's leg and yanked the man out of his saddle. Another prisoner picked up a stray brick from the ground and smashed the horse across the face. The creature toppled.

The officer rode the animal to the ground, but by then, the jig was up. The soldiers rounded on the attackers raising their weapons to their shoulders. One of the weapons cracked. The fourth prisoner lunged for the gunman and seized the muzzle. He locked it under his arm and the blast went past him without doing any harm.

Ida stood rooted to the spot watching the four attackers, the soldiers, the officer, and even the stricken horse transforming before her eyes. Their features distorted and deformed into monstrous visages of fangs, hatred, and bloodlust.

The soldiers outnumbered the attackers by a dozen at least, but at the same instant, as if at some unspoken signal, the whole column rose up and leaped on the soldiers. What appeared a few minutes before as an assembly of abject despair and hopeless weakness now erupted into a volcanic frenzy of killing and mayhem.

The prisoners, once so placid and submissive, laid into their captors with unimaginable fury. They changed into raging beasts more deadly and irrational than anything Ida saw in Ballantyne.

The whole scene exploded in a fraction of a second. The prisoners surged out of their ranks and overran the soldiers. Shrieks, screams, and roars of insane fury rose to a deafening cascade of confused noise.

Marvin yanked Ida by the arm to get her away, but there were too many prisoners. They stampeded the soldiers as one and swept the friends with them. Fear and alarm seared Ida's chest. Struggle as she might to get out of this trap, the crush of bodies forced her forward—closer to the soldiers.

Guns went off. She couldn't tell where they were coming from, but within seconds, she didn't need to know. Monsters seethed all around her and they didn't confine themselves to attacking the soldiers. They turned on each other grinning and slashing their fangs on all sides.

A grizzled fiend with a massive mouth of bloody spikes hurtled toward her head. Without thinking, she stuck her hand into her chemise and yanked out her pistol. She pointed it and fired straight into the thing's forehead. Its skull exploded and sprayed pulp and goo all over her face.

She ran her wrist across her eyes and cast a hasty glance around her. She had six bullets in this gun and that was one of them gone. She had to use this weapon to get her out of here, but when she searched her surroundings, she didn't see Marvin or any of her friends. They were all gone and she was completely alone.

She spun back the other way. Another monster soared out of the mix extending its horrible claws to grab her. She didn't fire this time. She cocked her arm across her neck and smashed the thing down with the pistol grip.

The creature went down shrieking and the noise attracted the attention of other demons nearby. They all rounded on her at once. This couldn't go on. She had to get out of here.

She took a hint from the prisoners and snatched a crooked stone from the ground. She bashed it right and left. She no longer cared what she hit. She went into a blood furor trying to kill as many of these creatures as possible. She lost all awareness of who or what or where she was or why she had to kill them.

She screeched in blood-fueled rage. Her hair whipped across her face and stuck in the blood and brain and muck stuck to her cheeks. She saw herself spinning into something close to madness. She *was* mad. She was monstrous, but she didn't care. In fact, she enjoyed it.

She let herself go in the insanity of changing into a monster—a monster who fed on death and destruction. She came upon a monster in a uniform and she fell on him in an ecstasy of cruel revenge. She didn't waste any bullets on him. She discovered him attacking another monster in a ripped dress.

She flew at the soldier from behind and delivered a punishing blow to the back of his head. He went down and she pounced. She landed in a crouch on his chest and pulverized his skull. She kept at it long after she left nothing recognizable of his head and most of his neck.

A guttural roar made her look up from her revelry. She caught sight of a huge monster with a mane. Gory fur surrounded a countenance warped by lethal passion. He rocketed at her so fast she couldn't defend herself.

He collided into her with the force of a freight train and ripped her off the dead soldier. His momentum carried them both several feet before he pounded her down on the pavement.

He stood on top of her and raised his claws to deliver a killing blow. She lifted her rock, but that wouldn't do any good against a foe this big. Instinct brought her gun around. She aimed it at his head. He gave a bone-shaking bellow and flexed for the final assault when the gun went off.

The enormous monster pivoted and the bullet punched into his chest. His thunderous roars vibrated the street beneath Ida's back. The impact hurled the creature backward and he landed hard.

Ida vaulted to her feet and sprang to follow up her victory. She bared her fangs and shrieked her war cry. She brandished her rock and flew at him to finish the job. She sprang on top of him and landed straddling his chest.

She actually let go of her pistol and grabbed the rock with both hands to bring it down on his face when she saw him beneath her. It was Marvin. Blood matted his hair and beard, but he wasn't a monster anymore. He stared up at the sky with blank, unseeing eyes.

Ida stared at him and all the fury and murderous hatred drained from her. She saw herself as she had been a few minutes ago and her stomach turned. She shot Marvin. She went so far over to becoming something inhuman that she shot Marvin.

His chest lurched when he tried to cough. She scrambled off him and dropped her rock in a hurry. She didn't want to touch it. She fell on Marvin and tried to pick him up. God, what was she thinking? How could she let this happen?

"Get up, Marvin!" she panted. "Oh, God, please don't let him be dead. Please, Marvin. I need you to get up." A sob cracked her voice. "Oh, please, Marvin, I need you! It's me, Ida."

He sagged in her arms and she almost burst into tears. How could she do this? How could she shoot a good man who did so much to bring her back to herself? She grappled to get a hold of him, but he weighed too much for her to lift.

All at once, he surged upright in her arms. He shot up into a sitting position and coughed again. "Marvin!" she screeched. "Can you get up, Marvin? Oh, please, don't be dead!"

He growled. "I'm not…. not dead…yet."

She moaned again, half in relief and half in shattered grief that she actually shot him. She could shoot herself for that, but right now, he needed her. He didn't stand up. Instead, he folded from the waist and flopped almost to the ground again.

She grabbed his shoulders and fought to straighten him up. "Come on, Marvin," she choked. "We're getting out of here."

She wedged herself under his armpit, but he was still too heavy for her to lift. He heaved onto one knee trying to help her, but even then, it took way too long to get him up.

She scrambled to get hold of her weapon. Monsters whizzed and howled all around her. She huddled close to Marvin as if he could somehow protect her from them.

With another heroic effort, she propelled him to his feet. He swayed and tottered, but with her straining every muscle, he managed to stay upright. She lurched forward and they staggered through the chaos going…somewhere.

Ida glanced right and left, but she didn't see any sign of the rest of the friends. They might be dead in this den of fiends. She wouldn't be surprised. Now she had to get herself and Marvin to safety at all costs.

Marvin's weight fell on her more than once. He took all her effort not to let him fall over. They pushed their way through countless monsters. Ida couldn't tell anymore who was a prisoner and who was a soldier—not that it mattered. One monster was as good as another.

Monsters packed the street from wall to wall. At the very farthest edge, another smashed building opened into what must once have been a nice foyer. Black-and-white checked tiles covered what was left of the floor and a carved paster ceiling ended at a torn-off edge of broken timbers.

Ida sank onto the ground and Marvin fell out of her arms. He flopped onto his stomach and hauled himself to the nearest wall. Ida did her best to pull him into a sitting position. "I'm so sorry! Oh, my God, can you ever forgive me? I didn't mean to! I didn't know it was you! I was out of my mind."

She tried to peel the bloody shirt away from the wound, but he slapped her hand away. "Quit fussing, girl. I'm fine."

"Fine! I shot you in the chest. Oh, mercy, how bad is it?"

He snarled again and pushed her hands away a second time. "It's a scratch. I hit my head when I fell. That's all." He cleared his throat and scooted up a few more inches. "Those monsters are pretty tough, I guess—a lot tougher than we are."

Once he got into a real sitting position, he pulled the collar of his shirt open. She stared at the spot on his upper shoulder where the bullet struck him. He smeared the blood away and she saw that he was right. The wound didn't penetrate through the muscle. She could see the torn flesh and it wasn't bleeding anymore.

She collapsed next to him. "Are you.... are you sure you're all right?"

He thrust out his hand and clasped hers. "If I change into one of those things again, you have my permission to shoot me a dozen times, especially if I'm trying to hurt you. In fact, I demand that you do just that. Understand?"

Her throat tightened and she grabbed his hand with all her strength. "Okay. You got it."

He cracked a crooked grin. "Now come on. We got somewhere to be."

They both stumbled to their feet, but when they stood up and looked out at the street, the monsters surged toward their building. Countless monsters charged the foyer all screeching and slashing at once.

Marvin pivoted to block Ida from them, but before either of them could move, a monster heaved out of the crowd carrying the biggest gun Ida ever laid eyes on. The monster was wearing a tattered rag of a dress, but her glowing, hateful eyes saw only blood.

The fiend aimed her cannon—or whatever it was—into the foyer. For a second, Ida gazed down a cylindrical tube to a small, round projectile far down the hole. The monster grinned showing all her deadly teeth and then her knobby fingers closed around the trigger.

Marvin slammed his palm into Ida's shoulder and sent her spinning away as the missile released and corkscrewed into the building. His strangled yell split the din. "Run!"

Then the blast ripped the building apart and sent her cartwheeling away.

# Chapter 12

**M**arvin came to his senses and faltered onto his hands and knees. His chest still hurt something awful where Ida shot him, but at least he could think straight. The furious thirst for blood, death, and destruction no longer clouded his thoughts.

He steadied himself against a wall and got his legs under him, but when he turned around to search for her, he discovered his worst nightmare coming true before his eyes. Monsters poured into the building.

He caught a moment's glance of Ida's head bobbing above the horde as they carried her out of sight at the far end of the foyer. He dove into the mix trying to fight his way to her. "Ida!" he roared. "Ida!"

"Marvin!" She waved her arms above her head, but she didn't seem to be walking. Her feet didn't touch the ground. The monsters drove her backward against her best efforts to stay where she was.

The creatures in front of him clawed and snapped and assailed each other as hard as ever. They didn't notice half of what they were doing.

He spotted a head of brown hair far out in the crowd. A human hand flailed into view and it clutched a gun in normal human fingers. Sheriff Oliver's clean-cut visage floated past Marvin's eyes and vanished.

"Sheriff!" Marvin bellowed. "Sheriff!"

The sheriff didn't hear him. No one could hear a thing with all these screeching demons blocking the way. Ida. He had to reach Ida. He had no idea where they would take her, but he had to find her.

He waded into the sea of monsters. One of them scratched him across the ribs and he rounded on the creature in a rage. He almost lost control again, but he forced himself to focus. Ida. Ida was more important.

The crowd swept him in her direction, but at the last second, the monsters turned and started swarming up the curving staircase toward a landing overlooking the foyer. Marvin thought fast and kicked out one of the banister's wooden staves. It cracked at the base and he seized it in both hands.

He used it to club away any monster that came near him, but by that time, they were already flooding the landing. They wheeled in all directions and rushed into bedrooms to carry out their mission of wholesale destruction there, too.

Marvin cast one more look around. Sheriff Oliver was in this river of bodies somewhere. If only Marvin could find him, he wouldn't be facing this army of monsters alone.

Another monster bit his arm. The teeth touched his skin and he reacted in a heartbeat. He whirled around and stove in the creature's head, but Ida dominated his every thought. She left no room for him to get angry at these senseless fiends. They didn't know what they were doing. He experienced that for himself.

Ida. Only Ida mattered. Just then, the throng carried him past one of the nicer bedrooms. The monsters inside were ripping the four-poster bed to scrap, but through the far window, Marvin saw Ida dangling by her arm. He couldn't see what was holding her up—if anything.

Marvin sprang into the room. He had to battle his way through dozens of monsters trying to attack him and each other and the furnishings all at once. He clubbed them aside and rushed the window.

He stuck his head and shoulders through. He thrust out his arms to catch Ida. "Ida! Grab on to me!"

"Marvin!" she screeched.

Far up in the sky, a dozen monsters dangled from the roof. They held onto each other's wrists in a chain of bodies with Ida twirling from the end. The wind caught her petticoats and billowed them in the breeze to show her chaps. She kicked and tried to fling her free arm upward to grab the monster holding onto her wrist.

The monsters chortled and chattered in glee at their ingenious trick. Their jerky movements kept twisting Ida out of Marvin's reach. Once, he caught hold of her petticoats and tugged her toward him, but before he could get a hold of her, the monsters started pulling her upward. The creatures at the top lifted the ones beneath and Ida rose out of his reach.

He tossed his club into the bedroom and stretched both arms as far as he dared. "Ida! Ida, come back!"

"Help me, Marvin!" she shrieked. "Help!"

The monsters raised her to the next story. She was way beyond his grasp now. He had to get her. These stupid fiends might drop her to her death on the pavement below.

He ducked back into the bedroom to find his club gone. He didn't care. Another monster charged him, but he kicked the thing away without mercy. Ida. Ida alone mattered now.

He barreled out of the bedroom and collided with Sheriff Oliver on the landing. The two men grappled each other in desperation. "Ida!" Marvin roared.

"Sadie!" Sheriff Oliver yelled back.

Marvin froze. "Where?"

"Where is she?" Sheriff Oliver hollered at the same time.

"The roof!" Marvin replied. "Where's Sadie?"

"Up the stairs."

The two men ran off together. Marvin kept a firm grip on Sheriff Oliver's arm and he felt the sheriff clutching him just as hard. Neither wanted to let go of the other.

They came up against another stampede of monsters on the stairs. Every monster in this crazy world must be inside this one building. He and Sheriff Oliver started fighting their way through the horde, but it wasn't so easy without the club.

They gained the next story. Marvin darted into a deserted bedroom, but when he looked through the window, Ida was almost on the roof.

He found Sheriff Oliver in bloody battle against a dozen monsters pinning Sadie to the ground. One of them darted its fangs for her throat to tear her in half. Sheriff Oliver lunged for the creature and crammed his weapon into the fiend's mouth. The gun went off and the monster's head vaporized in a cloud of blood spray.

Marvin pounced on the creatures piled on top of Sadie. He kicked and ripped them off. He flung their bodies over the banister to the tiled floor below. He sensed himself slipping into a rage, but he couldn't let Sadie go down.

One after another, he cleared her body while Sheriff Oliver blasted his gun at one monster after another. Marvin didn't want to think about where Sheriff Oliver got that weapon in this chaos. The sheriff emptied his gun until the two men met somewhere near Sadie's waist.

Marvin grabbed her. "You okay, girl?"

She wheezed so fast she couldn't speak. He set her on her feet and checked her to make sure she wasn't injured. She looked around with unseeing eyes. Her mouth opened and closed again and again without making any noise.

Sheriff Oliver tossed his gun away and pulled a different one from his belt. It wasn't a six-shooter or any other gun Marvin recognized, but as long as it could shoot, he didn't care. "Get up to the roof. I'm going to look around for the others and then I'll be right behind you."

Marvin didn't wait to be told twice. He leaped up the stairs two at a time. He ran all the way to the top. He didn't have to search for a way to the roof. He followed the steady stream of monsters all rushing the same way.

They blockaded the one door leading outside. Sunshine shone through the opening and more heads bobbed across the flat roof, but he didn't see Ida anywhere. These demons better not have hurt her or he really would lose it.

He snatched monsters from in front of himself and pitched them aside. He catapulted onto the roof searching everywhere for Ida. It took him a minute to find her.

Monsters waged their blood war all over the roof. They must have come up here to fight each other. He couldn't think of any other reason. They wrestled and slashed and ripped each other limb from limb. Some used weapons. Others used debris they picked up from anywhere.

In that moment, Marvin beheld the same otherworldly chaos unfolding that he'd seen inside the bubble. Random tools, stray trash, inanimate objects, and disembodied weapons with no hand wielding them came to life and attacked the monsters as furiously as they attacked each other.

A garden spade rotated past Marvin's head. It turned several revolutions and embedded its sharp edge in a monster's back. The creature crumpled where it stood. It never saw what struck it down. The spade gave a few frustrated jerks before it freed itself and went twirling off somewhere else.

An unmistakable shriek alerted Marvin to his mission. Three monsters hoisted Ida above the crowd. She floundered for a second and then they dropped her into the mayhem. He lost sight of her, but he'd seen enough.

He dove into the mix kicking and scratching his way through the horde. The monsters tried to fight him off, but they were too busy attacking each other to do much. Marvin worked his way between bodies until he could see Ida right in front of him.

Her skirts slapped back and forth with the tremendous effort of holding the monsters at bay. She spun one way fighting them with an iron bar in one hand and a hearth shovel in the other.

She brandished both in white-knuckle fists. She hacked the shovel across a monster's face and slashed to the bone. The creature whipped sideways with an anguished shriek, but she was already pirouetting back to her left to stove in another creature's head with the bar.

She bared her teeth and bellowed like an animal, but she didn't turn into a monster. Marvin didn't see her as a monster, anyway. She was magnificent and beautiful in her deadly rage. She struck down her enemies without quarter and she wore their blood as a badge of honor.

Out of the chaos, a kitchen cleaver came somersaulting straight for her. She saw it a fraction of a second too late before it embedded itself in her skull. She didn't have time to block it. She ducked and it thunked into another monster rising to pounce on her.

Marvin plunged into the monsters shoving them out of the way. He battled his way to her. She raised her iron bar to break his head open, but when she saw him, her face lit up.

Neither had time to celebrate their ill-fated reunion. At that moment, something sprang onto Marvin's back from behind. A jointed, clammy arm hooked around his neck and jerked him away from Ida.

She jumped forward to grab him. She called out his name, but at the same time, another four monsters converged on her from both sides. She clubbed one away with her shovel, but the others caught her and started muscling her toward the roof's edge.

She shrieked even louder. Marvin lurched to help her, but what felt like hundreds of monsters assaulted him from behind. He stuck out his arm. "Ida—no!"

Her rising screeches set his teeth on edge, but he couldn't reach her. The monsters yanked him over backward and he crashed onto his back.

He looked up at dozens of monsters piling on top of him. Their hideous faces grimaced and snarled and spat in his eyes. They clawed and sliced and pricked at him all over. They pinned him down so he couldn't rise. He could hardly fight them to save his own life.

A mouth full of teeth darted for his throat. He delivered a devastating punch to the massive jaws. The head snapped aside only for another three similar mouths to come at him from every side. He couldn't keep them all straight. There were just too many of them.

Something stabbed into his leg and the pain sent him exploding out of his mind. The needle blade sliced into the muscle and hot blood gushed down his thigh. He lashed out punching, kicking, choking—anything he could to drive these devils back.

Every time he made contact with one of them, another five took its place. He smashed faces and broke bone—at least, he hoped he did. He couldn't tell if he did any damage to them at all. They all looked the same now.

A hand shot out of nowhere and long, bony fingers closed around his neck. They choked him until he couldn't breathe. At the same time, five more monsters stood on his chest. The agony drove him insane, but he never quit fighting. He would fight until the end. He had to.

His vision swam and his eyes went dark. Lack of air made him fight all the harder, but he saw himself sinking. In a minute, he would pass out and then he wouldn't be able to stop them from tearing him apart. They would kill Ida, too. They would die here. They would never see Ballantyne or their friends again.

All at once, the hand around his throat ripped away. Blood rushed to his brain and his eyes snapped open. For half a second, he looked up at the clear blue sky dotted with fluffy clouds. He didn't see any monsters.

The next instant, the horde crashed in on him in all their fanatical mania. They rocketed inward to a point above his head, but they didn't attack him. He lunged off the roof and five monsters soared past him flying the opposite way.

Matilda straddled his knees planting her stout legs into the roof. Her blood-stained skirts brushed Marvin's knees and her thick arms quivered as she swung a sledgehammer in a brutal arc to club the monsters off.

Another raft of the demons hurtled inward to rend her limb from limb. She clenched her bulging jowls, cinched her fingers around the hammer handle, and swung. The monsters fell away in swaths.

"Get up, Marvin!" Matilda bellowed. "Get up!"

Marvin scrambled to his feet, but his injured leg refused to obey him. He dragged it across the roof to where he'd last seen Ida. Matilda cast terrible glares over her shoulder and backed up to defend him with crushing swings of her hammer.

The monsters launched one assault after another, but none of them could get past her. The more effectively she defended herself, the more monsters noticed that someone was standing up to them. They gathered from all over the roof and more flooded into view from the stairs.

Marvin didn't like leaving her to fight them alone, but her intention was clear. She kept her back to him and cleared a path while he worked his way toward Ida.

Her screams came from behind a glut of fiends right at the roof's edge. He snatched one creature after another by the neck and tossed them over the side. He enjoyed a sadistic thrill of listening to their petrified screams getting fainter as they fell to the street below.

He got rid of twenty of them before he found seven monsters lowering Ida and several more of their fellows over the side the way they did before. They made a chain of five monsters with Ida suspended from the end.

"Ida!" he thundered. "Hold on!"

"Marvin! Help me!"

"Hold on!" he yelled.

She screamed again, but he couldn't exactly throw *these* monsters over the side. He laid into the group anchoring the chain, but he didn't dare to unseat them.

He seized one creature by the shoulders and heaved the thing backward. Four more came with it and they all rounded on him to defend themselves. The ones anchoring their fellows started to let go of the chain.

The demons hanging off the end of the line jerked downward and almost fell. The monsters screamed as loud as Ida when they realized this amusing little game wasn't working out the way they planned.

Three of the anchormen launched at Marvin, but he wasn't paying attention to them anymore. He pushed them aside and jumped on the last three in the pile. He grappled for the wrist belonging to the first link in the chain. He grabbed and held on.

The seven anchor monsters rushed in to stop him from stealing their thunder. They ripped Marvin away and almost loosened his hold on the chain. They clamped his neck and did their best to haul him away from the edge.

He strained every fiber to stay where he was. He welded his belly to the rooftop and refused to budge. He crushed that monster's wrist in an unbreakable grip.

The monsters on the roof hurtled in to join the struggle, but Matilda stood guard and smashed them down with colossal hammer blows. Her primal bellows drifted to Marvin's ears. If she could stand strong under that assault, he would do the same thing.

He narrowed his eyes against everything. Stabs, cuts, and scratches assailed him all over. He felt his leg bleeding, but the pain only fired his rage to fight all the harder. He vented every scrap of his remaining strength to hoist the chain upward toward the roof.

The monsters' shrieks alerted the members of the chain that a fight was going on above them. They looked up, and when they saw Marvin holding them instead of their friends, they all swarmed up the chain to lay into him, too.

The last member of the chain let go of Ida. She screeched and twirled grappling to hold on. She managed to rotate just far enough toward the building that, when the monster released his hold on her, she fell against a windowsill.

Marvin found himself holding onto five monsters all scrambling to scratch his eyes out. They climbed over each other's heads and shoulders, each one trying to reach him first. Their grotesque visages leered in his face until he could see nothing but fangs.

He batted them aside trying to catch a glimpse of Ida, but the creatures didn't give up that easily. They vaulted at him only to fall and fly at him again and again.

In the end, he had to ignore the last two who perched on his shoulders. One laced its fingers around Marvin's head trying to tug his skull off his neck. The other looped gangly fingers under Marvin's armpits and tried to manually drag Marvin off the roof. The creature didn't seem to realize that, if it succeeded, *it* would fall to his death along with Marvin.

Marvin elbowed the first one a few inches sideways so he could see Ida. She clung to the building wall and balanced on the windowsill. In that moment, he got a clear view of the city streets spread out below him, but it wasn't the foreign city anymore. He was back in Ballantyne.

He lay on the roof of the Senator Hotel. He could see the jail, the saloon, the dry goods store, and the church inside the bubble. The blasted storefronts of Main Street extended to the courthouse on the left and the post office on the right.

It didn't flicker back and forth and it didn't return to the foreign city. It stayed Main Street. It was Ballantyne—or as close to Ballantyne as Marvin could ever hope it to be.

Ida's screams woke Marvin from his trance. The wind billowed under her petticoats and threatened to rip her off the windowsill. "Ida!" he called. "Ida! I'm here!"

"I can't hold on, Marvin! I'm gonna fall!"

"Hold on, Ida! We're going to get you. Matilda's here with me and Sheriff Oliver is inside. We'll get you off there!"

"Hurry, Marvin, please!" Her voice cracked. She peeked over her shoulder at the drop to the street. Then she buried her eyes against her shoulder. "I can't hold on much longer."

"Can you get through the window? Can you climb down enough to get inside?"

"The room is full of monsters. I don't dare!"

Marvin swallowed hard. If only he knew where Sheriff Oliver was, he might direct the sheriff to Ida's window. The sheriff could clear the room and then guide Ida inside, but Marvin didn't want to chance leaving her alone. She might fall while he was running around hunting for the sheriff. He might as well go to her window himself…. if only he knew which one it was.

Matilda bellowed behind him again and a powerful smash punctuated the monster's shrieks. Marvin had to think of something and quick. The monsters all over him didn't make it easier.

He cast around for something he could lower for her to hold onto. He'd give his right arm for a rope right now, but he couldn't go looking for that, either. In his last act of desperation, he took the only thing available.

He arched back his arm and grabbed the first thing that came to his hand, which was a monster. He ripped the creature off his shoulder. The thing's claws ripped Marvin's shirt, but he was too far beyond caring.

The creature flapped and struggled in his hands, but Marvin shook the thing over the drop until the monster squeaked and howled in terror. Marvin flipped it around and grasped it by one ankle.

The monster screeched louder than ever, but every time it tried to resist, Marvin shook it harder. He shook it until it jerked straight downward against his grip. He consolidated his hold on its ankle and flung the body toward Ida.

"Grab her, you filthy piece of trash!" Marvin roared. "Grab hold of her if you want to live!"

The creature shrieked itself hoarse. It fought with a vengeance, but when Marvin refused to let it go, it finally stretched itself out straight and extended a spindly arm toward Ida.

She was too far away for it to reach. It twisted to grimace up at Marvin, but Marvin's patience was already tattered paper-thin. Lightning quick, he took hold of the other monster. This time, when he jerked it free, its razor claws scored his neck. Every ounce of pain racking Marvin's body propelled him to fight even harder.

He tiptoed his fingers up the creature's shoulder to its neck. His fist closed around the thing's throat and he yanked. The monster pivoted into mid-air with a spine-chilling scream and Marvin caught it before it pinwheeled off into the beyond.

The thing twisted and convulsed in his grasp, but he shook that one as hard as the first. "Down!" he snarled. "You hear! Get down!"

The thing rolled its eyes and made faces, but when he gave it another brutal shake, it settled down. He jerked it toward its friend—the one that had just been helping this creature try to throw Marvin off the roof.

"Get down there!" Marvin thundered. "Get down there, or I swear to High Heaven, I'll drop you both. You got that! Get down there, and if you don't get her, it's *your* head! Understand?"

They understood, all right. They quaked in his hands. He would have done a lot worse, but he was all done playing games with these things. He shoved the second one toward its friend and it grasped the second monster's body in a death grip.

The first one clambered down his friend inching toward Ida. Every time they hesitated, he shook them again and made them scream in fright. They were a sight more afraid of him than they were of their friends. Marvin had to remind himself that these monsters were really just people. They had as much drive to save their own lives as normal people.

The first monster inched his way down to his friend's head and the two monsters locked wrists. The first one lowered himself until he dangled by his friend's arm and he stretched out toward Ida.

"Grab her!" Marvin ordered. "Grab her and pull her away from the building. I swear to Christ, if you drop her, you're going with her!"

The monster's bony arm migrated through space. He extended his long, clawed fingers toward Ida, but she hid her face and refused to take the hand.

"Grab hold, Ida!" Marvin called. "Come on! We'll pull you up!"

She still didn't move. The monsters struggled against the tow of gravity. Marvin had to grab his own monster with both hands to stop the creature from jerking out of his grasp.

"Ida! Grab on! You can do it. Take his hand, Ida. I won't let you fall!"

She whimpered something he didn't hear. Then, with a sudden leap, she sprang off the windowsill and launched herself for the nearest monster. The creature lunged for her at the same time and she almost soared straight past him.

At the last second before she plummeted to her death, the monster splayed all his arms and legs. He tossed himself away from the building and his unnatural fingers closed around her arm. She dropped through his grip and his hand jerked against her wrist.

She screamed something awful, but there she was, suspended above Main Street. The town seethed with thousands of monsters. Where they all came from, Marvin couldn't imagine.

The minute her arm locked in the monster's grasp, Marvin leaned back. He heaved his captive up to the roof. The two creatures almost let go of Ida again in their haste to reach safety, but in the end, Marvin hauled one and then the other over the side.

The second one pawed its way back onto Marvin's shoulder and Marvin flung his hand down to seize hold of Ida. She squeaked and panted for every breath. She caught his arm in both hands and held on with everything she had.

Marvin had to pause there and gather his resolve for the last inch of effort. He had her. He wouldn't let her go, but his arms and shoulders ached. He felt his strength ebbing from loss of blood.

He wasn't sure he could stand upright once he got her onto the roof. With only Matilda defending his back, he already knew they would have to fight their way out of the hotel.

They would have to fight their way out of town before they got anywhere near safety. All their grand ideas about bringing down the bubble and saving the town had come to nothing.

Ida stared up at him from below. Her huge eyes searched him for the strength and resolve to save her and he found it for her. He braced his one good leg against the roof and strained his arms to pull her up.

Now that she saw a friendly face above her, her fear faded. She swung toward the building and kicked to find some toehold against the walls. She tried to help him. She found a protruding nail and wedged her boot against it to lever herself up.

Marvin towed her high enough that he could catch her by the elbow and then by the armpit. He had his hands on her body now. Another few inches and she would flop down next to him as safe as anyone could be in this crazy town.

She grappled her fingers around his arms and shoulders pulling herself into his grasp. Her breath brushed his cheek when, without warning, ten cruel razors shredded his injured leg to the bone. He screeched in agony as the claws ripped from his thigh all the way down to his calf. His hold on Ida loosened against his best efforts to maintain it.

She flung one arm over his back, made a grab for his belt, and missed. Her weight fell out of his arms. At that moment, something grabbed him by the shoulders and flipped him over. He looked up at four grinning monsters on top of him, his life's blood saturating their claws.

Ida's scream tore his world apart. She fell backward off the roof and her fingers stripped down his arm. Her weight fell against his wrist and yanked his arm backward. The tendons holding his shoulder to his torso tore out and his shoulder dislocated with her hanging by the torn muscle alone.

One of the monsters lunged for his throat. Marvin couldn't move to defend himself. Every fragment of his attention focused on stopping Ida from falling. Even now, her twisting movements blasted him apart with splitting pain, but he held on through everything. He would still be holding on when the monsters killed him.

The monster cracked its menacing jaws to tear his face off when Sadie popped into his view. Where did she come from? She sprang upward in front of his eyes, stabbed a pistol into the monster's head, and pulled the trigger.

The monster's skull evaporated in a starburst of blood, brain, and bone. The cloud hardly dissipated when Sadie rotated sideways and shot the next monster through the ear. The other creatures rounded on her. She pinched her lips in an annoyed kind of sneer and crammed the gory barrel into the first mouth that opened for it.

The bullet exploded the monster's head and the other one shrieked in fury. It charged her spreading its dripping fangs wide to bite her in half. Quick as a thought, she stuck the gun under its chin and pulled the trigger.

She shut her eyes against the spray of debris covering her face, hair, and dress, but she didn't seem to mind. When the headless body flopped at her feet, she turned her crystal blue eyes on Marvin. She looked as placid and collected as when she slouched against the saloon bar fending off drunken admirers.

Marvin stared up at her, too astounded to believe what just happened. A few feet away, Matilda still cleared the roof with herculean sweeps of her hammer. She cast furious glances behind her to make sure Marvin was okay.

Another ear-splitting screech from Ida made him turn over onto his chest again, but now he knew for certain he couldn't pull her up. His arm and shoulder had gone numb and he couldn't feel the fingers of the hand to which she clung for her very life. Only her own efforts stopped her from falling.

Marvin trembled. His body threatened to shut down any second now. He felt himself starting to lose consciousness. He couldn't even control his lips to tell her how much he wanted to save her. His mind swam.

She looked up at him. He could see the words forming on her lips. She wanted him to help her. She wanted him to pull her up and get her out of town. She wanted him to take her home to Granite Ridge where they would both be safe.

That wasn't going to happen now. He was finished and Sadie wasn't strong enough even to hold Ida up, much less pull her to safety. He couldn't think of one possible thing he could do to save her life.

Their eyes met and an overpowering wave of sadness and affection flooded him. He couldn't even tell her how he felt, now when he was about to lose her forever.

At that moment, a hurtling missile streaked across Marvin's line of sight. At first, he thought it might be a monster. In the blink of an eye, it struck Ida and he saw that it was a common housecat transformed into a twirling ball of fur, claws, and teeth.

It tangled once in Ida's dress and then catapulted away about thirty feet off the ground. The impact was enough to dislodge her hand from Marvin's arm. She clamped her fingers around his wrist, but the blow made her slip and her palm glided across his.

She dropped away, floundered to grab him, and failed. Their eyes remained locked as she plummeted toward the carpet of monsters fighting, killing, and trampling each other down below.

Her skirts whooshed upward and her hair curtained her face. Her mouth opened and a scream pealed across town—a scream like no other—a scream that branded itself into Marvin's memory for all time. The sight of her falling out of his grasp and plunging to her death imprinted itself into his mind so he could never forget it.

She shot her arms and legs forward to reach out from Marvin. Then she flung them outward to the points of the compass, but nothing could stop that terrible fall. The light of understanding dawned in her eyes and she knew exactly what was about to happen.

As she fell, a shimmering curtain of purple-pink sparkled down from the sky. As if matching her fall, the bubble rippled and dissipated around Ballantyne. It fell like a drape crumpling to the floor in slow motion.

Marvin stared in devastation at Ida slipping out of his life forever when, without warning, a lone figure vaulted out of the mayhem below. Reverend Sherman sprang over the heads of a dozen monsters. His polished shoes hurdled from one body to the next and he launched through space to reach Ida.

Reverend Sherman rocketed off three heads and soared upward spreading his arms wide. He collided into Ida with impossible force and both of them tumbled twenty feet sideways. They flew only a short distance before they started to fall.

Reverend Sherman grappled his fleshless arms around Ida's body and rotated himself backward. He spun her on top of him and fell spine first into the mob. Below him, the enormous, transfigured bull that first knocked Ida into the bubble looked up from the horde. His spiked horns pivoted upward and Reverend Sherman fell right on top of them.

They pierced his torso through the back and Ida toppled out of his arms. She hit the ground and somersaulted to her feet as the last twinkling light of the bubble drifted to Earth. It winked out and all the monsters changed back into people, animals, and lifeless sticks of wood.

The bull transformed back into a normal bull. He shook Reverend Sherman's ruined body off his curved horns, snorted at the body, and then trotted away through the streets.

# Chapter 13

Ida staggered over to Reverend Sherman's body and collapsed on her knees next to him. His whole chest was a mass of pulpy blood boiling out of a dozen holes in his ribcage. She touched his shoulder, but his lifeless eyes stared past her at something out of sight.

All over town, people stopped what they were doing and looked around them trying to grasp what they were doing here. Birds flew away and a few cats and dogs scampered for cover. Broken wood and tools scattered in the dust. Horses, cattle, and a few chickens shook themselves and moved off at a leisurely pace.

Up on top of the Senator Hotel, Marvin stared down at her with a blank expression. His mangled arm dangled over the side. While Ida watched, Sadie poked her head into view over his shoulder and then Matilda appeared on his other side.

The two women studied Ida and their eyes widened when they saw Reverend Sherman's body. Then they got hold of Marvin and eased him onto the roof where Ida couldn't see him.

Ida scanned the town hardly daring to believe that everything returned to normal so fast. What caused the bubble to evaporate like that? She couldn't think of any reason, but it was gone. The friends certainly hadn't been in contact with each other when it happened. She had been holding onto Marvin's arm just before, but she wasn't touching him when the bubble came down.

The people around her either didn't remember or chose not to react to what they'd just been doing. They wandered off to their own business. They stepped bodies littering the street as though the bodies weren't there.

Ida looked down at Reverend Sherman again. He saved her life. He sacrificed himself and took the bull's horns in her place. Did that have anything to do with dispelling the bubble? How could it? The bubble burst before he died.

Just then, Sheriff Oliver rushed out of the hotel holding a pistol in his hand. He charged over to Ida and almost fell over gasping for breath. "Ida! You're alive! Jesus Christ, I thought you were dead."

"So did I." Why did she sound so calm? She should be distraught over this. "Reverend Sherman saved me."

Sheriff Oliver didn't seem to hear her, either. He squinted at the townspeople. "What's wrong with everyone? Don't they remember turning into monsters?"

"Maybe not. Help me get him into the church, will you please?"

Sheriff Oliver jolted alert. He took a second to realize what she was asking him, but when she bent over the body, he woke up from his daze. He tried to stick the gun into his holster, but it didn't fit. It was the wrong shape.

He examined it for a second and then decided to jam it into his belt. He crouched down and scooped up Reverend Sherman in his arms. Ida accompanied him toward the church.

Sheriff Oliver surveyed the bodies lying at odd angles all over town. "I suppose we'll need to get these people buried in a hurry."

"No one seems in a rush to claim their loved ones," Ida remarked. "Everyone cleared out as soon as the bubble came down."

"I can't blame them. No one wants to admit they were part of it."

"They'll have to if they want to claim their dead."

She opened the church door and held it wide for Sheriff Oliver to angle Reverend Sherman's body into the aisle. He carried the preacher to the steps leading to the pulpit. There was nowhere else to put him.

Sheriff Oliver laid the body on the middle step. Ida ducked into the vestry and came back with a woolen blanket. She draped it over Reverend Sherman and tucked it under his chin.

Then she and Sheriff Oliver stood back and stared down at the body. "What do you think made it come down?" Sheriff Oliver asked. "Was he right about it being something to do with touching each other?"

Ida shook her head. "It couldn't be. We weren't touching each other when it came down. None of us was. It started to fall when all of us were separated."

A moment's silence fell between them. The silent church throbbed with unnatural stillness after all the shrieking and screaming of just a few moments before. This silence didn't seem possible in a world where all those monsters lived. Were they real? Were any of the others wondering the same thing?

Sheriff Oliver turned toward her. "Have you seen Slim?"

"I was just about to ask you the same thing. I haven't seen him since.... well, since the column broke up. Sadie, Matilda, and Marvin are on the hotel roof. I saw them after...after Reverend Sherman died."

"Slim must have fallen. He's probably outside somewhere."

She glanced up and caught his eye. Then they both looked away. "How do you explain that city and that camp being the same as Ballantyne?"

Sheriff Oliver shrugged gazing down at Reverend Sherman. "I don't explain it. I don't think I even want to try."

"If there's no explanation for why the bubble came and why it disappeared, maybe it will come back."

"Maybe it had a time limit. How should I know? Reverend Sherman isn't here to explain it to us and I don't think he could even if he was. I'm only glad it's gone."

She looked behind her toward the door. What would she find out there? Would she and Sheriff Oliver walk out of this church into a swarming horde of monsters?

What if the bubble going away was an illusion—a cruel hallucination? What if the bubble wasn't gone? What if it would never go away and they were still inside it? What if there never was any way to break the bubble and get the world back to the way it was before?

She faced front to find Sheriff Oliver studying her. A question clouded his features. Was he thinking the same thing?

They turned and left the church without speaking. Without agreeing, they stopped on the threshold and observed Ballantyne returning to its normal routine—all except the bodies lying everywhere. Dust clung to them. Tumbleweeds bumped over them. Dogs sniffed them. Flies buzzed around them.

Superimposed over the too-quiet scene, Ida saw again the shadowy mayhem inside the bubble. Demons slashed, gnashed, killed, and ripped each other to shreds. Objects came alive and animals went mad.

In front of her eyes, three people crossed the street on their way toward the dry goods store. They glanced toward the church and squinted against the sun. For a second, Ida saw their features twisted and contort into monstrous grimaces.

Would she ever stop seeing the monsters everywhere she looked? Would her sight ever return to normal after what she'd seen?

Maybe Reverend Sherman was right and all these people really were monsters underneath their respectable disguises. They could change in a blink and their murderous tendencies would break the surface. They would become grinning fiends bent on mayhem and murder of those they loved most.

That same darkness lurked in her heart. The right combination of circumstances would release it—actually, the wrong combination of circumstances would. This really was Hell on Earth. She just didn't see it before.

The next minute, the three people stopped. One of them shielded their eyes against the glare and she recognized old Margaret Winslow, the laundress. She burst into a smile and gave Ida a cheery wave. The image of the monsters evaporated. This was Ballantyne, a sleepy little town populated by good people. There were no monsters here. If Ida thought about it the right way, she could imagine they never had been here at all. It was all her imagination.

# Chapter 14

I da gathered the eggs in her apron and bunched it in one hand while she scattered corn to the hens. She shut the coop door and hurried back to the house. She picked up the water bucket in her free hand and lugged it to the steps before she climbed into her clapboard cabin.

She bustled to the kitchen counter. She put the eggs in their basket as Marvin stumped in from the bedroom. He'd stayed there for the last week while he healed from his injuries.

Two long staves strapped on either side of his leg banged against the hardwood floor. He put his weight on them instead of his foot and he leaned on a crutch propped under his left armpit. His right arm hung in a sling.

He hobbled to the armchair by the fire and collapsed into it. He stretched his splinted leg in front of him with a groan. "Where's that Codger of mine? Don't tell me he's still sulking."

Ida laughed. "He's still under the barn. I saw him peeking out when I went to fix the water trough. He wagged his tail at me, but I don't think he'll ever forgive you for coming to stay here."

"He shouldn't complain. You feed him a sight better than I ever did even if he *is* ungrateful."

"Don't be too hard on him. He's had you to himself for years. It must be hard on a dog to get half-abandoned on a strange place and receive his handouts from a stranger's hand. He doesn't want me. He wants you."

"Hogwash! I went out there to practically beg him to come out—at great cost, I might add. The wretch wouldn't even look at me."

Ida had to laugh at the memory. "I know. I was there."

Marvin snatched the newspaper from its place by the fire. He flipped it open in a great show of dismissing Codger from his mind. He laid the paper out on his lap and turned the pages with his good arm. "If he can't at least adapt to the situation for my sake, he belongs under the barn. It isn't as though I asked to get injured and I wouldn't be able to feed him at all if I was laid up at my place."

Ida bit back a grin. She and Marvin had this conversation every morning about Marvin's distraught dog. The poor animal lurked under the barn day and night, even when Ida pushed dishes of food between the piles for Codger to eat. He just couldn't get used to this sudden and unexplained change in his circumstances.

Ida got busy making breakfast. She had plenty to do with Marvin staying at her place while he healed up. She managed both ranches, did all Marvin's chores, herded his stock to pasture each day, and patrolled his fence lines as well as her own.

She mixed up the biscuit dough and put the pan in the oven while she made gravy and fried bacon. She wouldn't go to such trouble only for herself, but she wanted Marvin to be comfortable and taken care of while he healed.

"Did you hear the news?" he called from his chair. "The Minnesota Congregation is sending us a new preacher."

Ida spun around and gasped. "When did you hear that?"

He flipped a page on his lap. "Sheriff Oliver told me. He showed up yesterday while you were over at the Wendell Draw."

"You didn't tell me he stopped by. What else did he say?"

"He said the Town Council wants us to appear before them to give a report on the bubble phenomenon. He said we don't have to go if we don't want to because he already gave them his report and talking about it won't do any good. He said he tried to talk them out of investigating it further because he feels that bringing it up and asking a million questions will only make everyone uncomfortable."

She propped her hand on her hip while she waited for the next batch of bacon to fry. "What you mean is that it would make the people who killed uncomfortable."

"What difference does it make? You and I killed inside the bubble. We killed living people. Anyway, he thinks that, if the Town Council is going to start asking questions, that will only lead to asking who killed whom and that's a losing proposition all around."

She turned back to the stove. "He might have a point there."

"Does that mean you won't appear? If you won't, I won't, either. Whatever we do, I think we should stand together—either for or against."

"I'm not against investigating, but Sheriff Oliver might be right that asking too many questions will only lead to hurt feelings and won't accomplish anything."

He turned another page. "You decide what you want to do and I'll do the same thing."

"If you want to appear, you should do it. We don't have to do the same thing."

"No," he declared. "We'll do the same, no matter what."

She shrugged and went back to her work. "Okay. I'll think about it."

The cabin went quiet except for the sizzle of bacon grease. Firewood popped in the stove. Unbidden, Ida's mind wandered back to that terrible day when the bubble appeared in town.

In the week since the great battle, she tried to put it out of her mind. She tried as far as possible to return to her normal life, but it wasn't easy. For one thing, Marvin's presence in her house offered a constant reminder of the sacrifice he and Reverend Sherman made that day.

Now the Town Council wanted to revisit the whole episode. She hoped to High Heaven they didn't intend to pursue legal action against anyone who participated in the killing. Sheriff Oliver was right that such a course would be a huge mistake.

Ballantyne needed to heal. Everyone needed to return to their normal lives. It was bad enough that nearly everyone in town had to bury someone they loved. Reverend Sherman's funeral was especially difficult for Ida and Marvin.

Sheriff Oliver was also right that, if the bubble ever came back, there wasn't a blessed thing anyone could do to stop it. Better to enjoy the peaceful time before then rather than dwelling on it.

"Listen to this!" Marvin read out an article in the paper. "'The world is buzzing with the news that a giant black bubble appeared in the sky over downtown Paris last week. It remained there for seven hours. It hung suspended a hundred yards above the ground without moving before it vanished without a trace. The following day, reports came in from eastern Prussia that an identical bubble materialized over Prague. It enveloped the city for three days before it disappeared without explanation. Experts and philosophers from all over Europe are gathering in Paris this week to discuss the phenomenon and come to some conclusion about what it means.'"

He looked up and his eyes met Ida's. They stared at each other and a chill struck Ida's heart. "When was that?"

He checked the top of the page. "This paper is six weeks old, so it would have happened seven weeks ago."

Ida swallowed hard, but her parched throat wouldn't make any sound louder than a whisper. "That's two bubbles in a week....before it ever showed up in Ballantyne."

"You know what this means, don't you?" Marvin shot her a wild grin as he turned the next page.

"No. What does it mean?"

"It means stay out of Paris."

<u>The End.</u>

# Keep Reading

## Onyx Series

You can find it at your favorite book retailer.

# Sign Up Once--Get all Theo Mann's free books including brand new releases

Lourdes, France, 1816

With food shortages and sky-high prices raging across France, tensions are running high as hunger and desperation drive the population to the breaking point.

Jean and Marie Albert just wanted to buy food for themselves and their young daughter. Little did they know a force more deadly would explode everything they thought they knew about reality.

When a mysterious bubble takes over the landscape and monsters roam the countryside killing everything in their path, Jean and Marie must fight with everything they have just to survive. Even survival might be asking too much as dark secrets from the past threaten their sanity, their love for each other, and everything around them.

Will the battle ever end? Will the world ever go back to the way it was?

When this is all over, these lost souls might just discover that some things are more important even than survival—some things that could turn monsters into angels and evil into good.

Sign up for the newsletter at www.theomann.com to read the book for free.

# About Theo Mann

I write 70 books per year—and yes, before you ask, all these books are my original creative work. Nothing written under my name is AI-generated or ghostwritten because I write better than AI and any ghostwriter out there.

People don't read fiction for entertainment or to escape from reality. People read fiction to see their humanity reflected in another person's character and story.

This is my promise to you. When you read my books, you'll see your own humanity reflected in the characters and stories. I take this commitment to my readers very seriously. My books are an intimate form of communication between us. I would never disrespect my readers by turning that over to a machine or another writer. This is my bond between me and you as my reader.

I write 20,000 words per day as my daily work output. If anyone with a public platform would like to challenge me to prove this in a controlled environment, feel free to contact me on this website's contact page. How do I do write so much? Find out more on my blog, *Crimes Against Fiction* at www.theomann.com.

I worked as a professional ghostwriter for fifteen years. Now I'm on a mission to set a Guinness World Record by writing 700 books over the next ten years and 1400 books over the next twenty years, all originally written by me.

See my website for the full book list. I'm also the author of *Proof for the Existence of God* and the *Crimes Against Fiction* blog.

If you have a story idea, or if you would like me to explore a series in more depth, or if you'd like me to explore a character by writing a spinoff series about that character or world, leave me a message on my website's contact page. I answer all reader emails, so ask me anything, tell me what you liked and didn't like, and let me know where you'd like your favorite series to go. I would love to hear your ideas and find out what you'd like to read next.

You can read my work for free on Royal Road @TheoMann.

If you enjoyed this book, please consider leaving a review. You can also support me on Patreon at www.patreon.com/InvisiblePublishing.

Find out more at www.theomann.com.

# Also by Theo Mann (so far)